The Last Will and Testament
of the Incredible
Mister Rutland Quincy Sherwood
A novel by Daniel Reed

Let your imagination soar...

For my dearest Charlotte, Levi, Graham, Benjamin, Asher and Abraham.

All my love Dan Dan

Chapter 1

Rutland Quincy Sherwood was by no means a man of expansive wealth and nor was he a peasant but if you were able to calculate a man's income simply by the life he lived then by God, he was the richest man in the world. Ever since he was a young lad, Rutland had a gift for finding the undiscoverable and if you hung around him long enough he would try to convince you that he and not Christopher Columbus actually discovered the land across the pond, known today as America. He was so good actually that he turned his desire to find, that which was hidden into a successful career of salvaging.

Most of his client's requests were simple, they would pay for the expedition and as long as he brought back the items they sought after, everything else found, he deemed worthy of possessing, he could keep. On occasion he would get some odd requests but his motto was "The stranger the acquisition in need the better the keep." He truly lived a life of finders-keepers.

There was no score too little or destination too far for Rutland and his band of misfits. To onlookers he was a myth, to his friends he was a legend and to his family he was always there, no matter where in the world his next prized possession found him. Unfortunately, he slipped into a coma five days ago, just shy of his ninety-sixth birthday, which brings me his fourth oldest grandnephew and family's second oldest lawyer to his humble abode. Amazingly enough Great-Uncle Rutland did not look a day over fifty, he always joked that the secret to his youthfulness was attributed to his sense of adventure. He was always telling me I needed to get out from behind the desk and paper work as I was twenty-nine going on ninety-two.

It was an odd feeling going over to his house today knowing that I wouldn't be greeted at the door with a wide smile or puzzling riddle.

No matter the occasion he always went above and beyond to make every person he encountered feel welcome but most of all he had ability of making you feel like you were themost important person in the world for however brief a moment.

I pulled my car into the drive way as far up as possible to leave room for the other heirs to park.

His house was tall, thin, with a shade of black, a slight tilt in the roof, a bright red door and a single flowerpot on the step that only held some soil. He had four sets of stairs from top to bottom accounting for three hundred sixty five and half steps as he saw it fit that each day of the year be another step towards destiny and on the occasional leap year he would take full advantage of the extra day. His quips were always a hodgepodge of well wishes, Irish proverbs and ancient sayings.

He wore a five o'clock shadow better than any man that ever lived. He maintained a healthy regiment of eating and exercise as well as a peculiar style about his wardrobe. The best way to put it, he was fashionably late by a century on occasion all-depending on the year you found him in. By year I mean room as each room had been designated a much different time, which was the theme for that rooms trinkets. Not every possession belonged to that time or place but every single item had its own place in time.

Which brings us to the reading of the last will and testament of; now he always made me promise shouldI write about his life that I use the word Incredible Mr. Rutland Quincy Sherwood.

The entire family gathered into the empty living room, which Rutland used for thinking and planning. As he never had children of his own, he sort of assumed the duty of a stand in father for his brother's family and my, would be grandfather, who passed away in the war. There sat my father Brunley Sherwood, his siblings Elizabeth Martin, Carter Sherwood and Marian Strider, their spouses my mother Pippen Sherwood, followed in order Sterling Martin, Rose Sherwood and Dean Strider. My cousins sat side by side with their parents at the ready to claim what was rightfully theirs as the great-nieces and nephews were being watched by the next oldest from myself who had just turned fifteen, in the room just beyond the kitchen.

"I Arthur Clive Sherwood hereby declare as the executor of the last will and testament of the Incredible Mr. Rutland Quincy Sherwood that the reading of such document will be followed by a family dinner before any of the possessions be split up." I cleared my throat. "Are there any objections before we proceed?"

Uncle Carter raised both of his hands

right as Auntie Rose put an elbow in his side. Truth was no one in the family beside myself, my father and mother have stepped foot in this house in years and they were lucky that they had been thought of at all. They were hoping to land a windfall but as the writer of the will I can tell you that in order to see it as such you would need to open your imagination to an entirely different meaning of the term rich. You see, Rutland found the most value, in his adventures, rather than the materialistic end of acquiring such rare items. I began to read...

"To all the loved ones I have ever held dearly and to the ones I wish I had held a little closer. May you find all of your hearts desires, in the rooms, I have designated for you. My will is to be carried out under the circumstance I am no longer able to have a cognitive reflex and should I not parish remain on life support until I wish to exhale my last breath.

To my dearest nephew Brunley and his beautiful bride Pip I leave everything in the room marked fourteen ninety two, may you find the time to explore the open seas before the good Lord calls you home."

The easiest way to explain the age gap in our family was that well, we were late bloomers in the bearing offspring department. It was odd but it worked for us.

"To my mischievous nephew Carter and his lack luster bride Rose, I leave you everything from the room at the top of the steps last door on the left, may you find the light you desperately are in need of."
As Rutland got older he minced his words even less.

"The top floor, are you kidding me!" Rose ungratefully blurted out as she rolled her eyes.

"To my naiveté niece Elizabeth and her scammer of a husband Sterling who is probably just here for the free food which he most certainly should cut back on. I leave you everything from the room on the second floor first door on the left and try not to get too wrapped up in it."

I could tell by the look on their faces no one was really amused by their inheritance. Only my parents seemed excited for their new nautical gear, which will look spectacular at their beach house. I am one hundred percent positive that everyone else were more worried about walking up the steps than actually receiving a piece of Rutland's legacy.

"To my talkative and well talkative is being nice, alright then obnoxious niece Marian and her well-mannered gentlemanly but unfortunate for him husband Dean, I leave to you everything in the cellar."

"Finally to my beloved grand-nephew Arthur, I leave you the keys to this house and order you to be the caretaker of such an estate as I am no longer capable of keeping up with the foliage.

As well as I leave you Merlin's key which can be found in the pocket of my favorite trousers that I am currently wearing with the help of my nurse… and should you figure out it's belonging, you may plunder all you find."

"And how come Arthur gets something and we don't?" My cousin Holly, Elizabeth and Sterling's only offspring, shouted in a childlike fit cutting me off from finishing the remainder of his will which were just legal terms for me.

At one point in our lives Holly and I were inseparable, but now a days she is busy husband shopping at the local universities social clubs with her horrid friends.

"Simple!" I replied. "His instructions made it clear that each family was to partake in the designated room, meaning that everyone gets something, as I begged him it would be the only way to keep World War Three from happening in this family. He added that last part for me after I left and sealed it himself for us to open on the very occasion he was not here to give us his possessions himself."

They didn't seem pleased with my answer

but it would be enough to get us through a peaceful meal, served to us by the one remaining housemaid. Merely seconds after dessert was served and coffee had been indulged in, they cleaned out every room without even saying goodbye. Leaving my father and mother and myself in peace and quiet for the first time in a week.

"So what are you going to do with the place? My mum asked.

"Well he left clear instructions not to change anything until he wakes up?" I replied.

My parents laughed as my father continued. "Yep, Uncle Rutland always lived his life on the hopeful side."

As much as I was with them on the doubtful side of his glorious awakening, He was turning ninety-six this year and everyday he was in a coma seemed to add a year to his appearance.

"Well I am going to keep it tidy and water the pot of soil out front as he requested, I am to reside in his guest quarters which is adequate enough work space for me given that I have decided to start my own firm, and it will be the perfect transition."

"That sounds absolutely splendid, my dear." Mum looked on in an unsure manner, as I was about to make partner with my current firm. I just didn't have the heart to tell her that the firm had closed its doors due to lack of clientele.

My Dad pulled me aside. "Look son, I know you and Rutland were close but do me a favor and be careful. His business came with a lot of friends but also enemies that sooner or later might just come looking for the very items he holds dearest. Best not to get involved in it and keep focused on your future."

My parents said their farewells for now as they loaded up their new belongings into a few totes. As I returned for my first night alone well not completely as the unconscious but still breathing body of the Incredible Mr. Rutland Quincy Sherwood lay just down the hallway.

A loud bang at the front door awoke me mid dream as I grabbed my glasses from the nightstand, followed by a morning robe. I was befuddled as to who would be at Rutland's house just shy of five thirty in the morning. I begrudgingly looked through the peephole as the beauty that bewitched the other side of the glass startled me. I quickly ran upstairs and put on trousers and a button-downed shirt, took a quick look at my hair before opening the door. She stormed right in and past me as if I wasn't even there.

"No time for introductions just point me to the direction of Rutland's room please." She said in a somewhat pleasant but still demanding manner.

"Just beyond the kitchen, follow the low hum of his ceiling fan." I said, as I was not too far behind. She was certainly on a mission of some sort. She removed her coat and pulled out a bag full of what appeared to be medical devices and none of which I have ever seen. Just as she was about to stick my uncle Rutland, I pulled her hand back. "Hold on just a minute, you. You cannot just barge in here with all your fancy tools and no explanation."

"Fair enough." She obliged. "My name is Eliza Dunmore and before I became your Uncle's Nurse, my mother attended to all of his peculiar health needs. So you could say I know Rutland better than almost anyone."

"Oh, well in that case, I am going to have to see some credentials." I said promptly.

"He thought you might ask me for some." She said wittingly. "So here goes, your name is Arthur, and you have planned out every day of your life since you were a wee lad. You have a cozy profession as a lawyer and by the looks of the boxes currently in the living room; it would appear you are venturing off on your own. You never had a serious relationship, as love is a part of the better half of your ten-year plan. You were Rutland's favorite person in the world outside of himself."

I won't lie this was the longest conversation I had with a lady outside of my previous secretary and even she was too old for me.

I couldn't hear past Eliza's radiant blonde waiving hair and velvet red lips, her blue eyes pierced my glasses as I could feel my blood pressure rising.

"He also said that you might pass out as you don't get out much in the way of socializing with beautiful women."

I woke up on the couch in the room next to Rutland's.

"Glad to see you are finally awake. It is about time we had a talk without you passing out." She said moving closer to me, handing over a glass of water.

She smelled of roses and fresh linen. She passed me a picture of her mother and Rutland. "You see Rutland and my mum were more than just friends as it were, oh they started out rivals actually and soon became partners and finally lovers. That was until my mum disappeared ten years ago. I then took on full responsibility as sort of Rutland's right hand woman."

At this point her beauty had worn off on me and I was able to listen more intently. It was all fascinating but very vague.

"He said you would be tough to convince. So he told me a story only you would be able to confirm. It is quite the tale actually, hard to believe that when you were fifteen you helped your uncle break into a museumto steal post war art that rightfully belonged to the widow of the artist."

I thought a moment. "You could have read about that in the papers though. You seem like someone who is well versed in the art of research as it were."

"One detail I left out, a security guard was about to make his rounds when you had to squeeze the last gate. You lost your trousers in the process and had to walk home practically naked." She finished.

I must admit that portion of the story wasn't in the papers and they never figured out whom those pants belonged to. That was the first and last time my parents let me work for Rutland. Truth was he never broke a law that didn't need bending because his heart was always in the right place, he salvaged for the good of others. It always begged the ethical question, is stealing from a thief morally wrong, and even considered stealing, when being returned to the rightful owner.

"By the way, that body in the other room is not Rutland, well it only would appear to be him." She spoke confidently. "You see, throughout the years my mum and Rutland plundered together.

They came across many unexplainable things and if they were to ever be stuck in a situation of sorts that would require an unorthodox form of rescuing, well I would be sent this with instructions."

She pulled out half of a key and placed it on the table.

I gave her a puzzled look. "The instructions were?"

"To come find you, you blockhead." She laughed. "My guess is you have the other half to this key."

I had totally forgot about the key Rutland said was in the pocket of his favorite pair of trousers, which he was currently wearing on account of his usual nurse helped him put them on. We checked the front two pockets until we realized nothing was ever normal with this man. It took the strength of us both to roll him over and retrieve the key from his back pocket. We set him along his back once more to rest until further investigation could be done.

We put the two pieces side by side and read the inscription together. "Unlock the way to find the things that wish to never be found and lock away all the things in secret without a sound." The two sides merged together with a glow as Eliza began to tell me the story her mum had told her as a child.

"This key belonged to a magic man of sorts, some would call him a wizard while others feared him to be the devil himself. To the ones who truly knew him he was just Old

Merlin. He sold elixirs of all sorts to all people of all kinds of propriety. One day his shop was broken into and all of his life's work was stolen in an instant. After three months of meditating and soul searching, he forged a door with a lock made from the gold that King Midas himself touched. That door had only one key to it, which was split into two parts and a spell cast over it to seal that which was lost behind it. Rumor has it that Rutland found that door and it is in this very house with treasures behind it that history thought was lost forever, lands that you never knew existed but only in fairytales." She spoke with such eloquence, but still I have seen every door in this house and none of the likes she described.

"So, you mean to tell me that Rutland could very well be alive?"

"It is possible that he is stuck in another time and another land far be it from here. But the longer he stays there, the more permanent his death here becomes."

"What are we talking here? Knights? Dragons? Evil king?"

"Probably all of it at this point. Where ever he is, the only way to him is to find the door."

We searched everywhere for the next four hours until just about giving up when I noticed that the painting in his empty living room, of himself no less was just about the right height and width of a slightly normal than large size door.

"Eliza, come quick and help me move this painting." I said as we both grabbed a side.

"And Lift!"

We placed the painting face down on the floor. It had been hanging on a false wall, which we then pushed back and slid off to the side. To our surprise there was the door Eliza had heard of since she was a little girl. I bent down and tried to peak through the keyhole before we took the key and together put it in the lock.

We said the inscription one more time for good measure and with our fingers crossed turned the key. We could hear the pins tumbling in the door, as it started to creek open. We entered the dark room in search of a light; I found the switch on the wall. To our surprise we were standing in a room easily three times the size of the house it was currently residing in. Apparently I passed out again as to when I woke up I found her standing over me flipping through one of the thousands of books that were in here. The artwork alone would be worth millions but still could you really even put a value on any of it. This was truly a one of a kind discovery with artifacts never seen by the likes of this present day.

"Can you believe it, the lost scrolls of the

Cinead?" She said with enthusiasm as I just nodded as if I knew what she was talking about.

"Legend has it that this city was known for its lavished farmlands until the sky rained down fire on its people for being ungrateful of the land they were given. Leaving nothing but desert to now survive as the remaining people took on the name Cinead, meaning born of fire."

"That is lovely, really brilliant but what are we currently looking for?" I said as the room was too large to simply tour, we had to begin digging.

"We are looking for a box said to have belonged to King Saul. It is but the first step in unlocking the where a bouts of Rutland and if I am lucky my mum."

"We are talking about the King from bible times? And this box will help us?"

"Yes and no the box itself is merely a container holding an item that we will most certainly need but first we need to find the box, because we need to figure out how to open the box but only after we find the box. Get it?" She said flippantly.

"Got it!" I said thinking to myself this woman was out of her mind. We searched high and low.

Languages I've never seen before on maps that had no geographical relevance to our current world. As she went on a rampage style finding mission, I being logical looked for the oldest books I could find hoping that one of them would lead me to some previously undiscovered biblical text that hopefully lead to the box itself. To my luck the box was sitting under two papyrus scrolls.

"Over here!" I yelled as she came flying over the shelf behind me.

"Did you find it?"

"I believe so but I can't make out any of the writing on the box."

"Let me take a look!" She grabbed the box from my hands. "Oh this is good, I have seen this language before." She pulled out a notebook with scribbles in it that only she could decipher. Almost two hours later she handed me the paper she had written on. "The wisdom you seek can only be unlocked by the one who slays giants."

Unfortunately for us, that counted us both out but there had to be more. I told her to flip the box over and on the bottom was an oval shaped dent with more writing.

Being that I processed what she initially translated I could read it without her help almost immediately. "The sling delivered a single stone and a victory to the king."

"He told me you were brilliant." She uttered as I basically decoded an ancient language after only being given one sentence as comparison. "But that was something on an entirely different level, and I don't impress easily."

We took the box from the room and made our way into the kitchen to figure out the riddle. I put on a pot of coffee as she scribbled away on paper. It wasn't until about my third cup of coffee that I realized I had figured it out. I put the paper from last week on the table. Headline read, "London Museum to host an Artifact Exhibit of Biblical Proportions opening April 30th. Followed by a list of items to be on display, including parts of the Ark built by Noah, the Holy Grail, Moses' staff, the silver of Judas betrayal and the stone of David which has been confirmed by many sources to be the exact one he struck down Goliath with."
Eliza stood up in a hurry and kissed me on the forehead while making her way towards the door. "Excuse me, and where are you off to in a rush?"

"I am going to case the place to see if it is a one or two person heist, while you go about your day as normal to not raise suspicion of what we have just recently discovered. Is that alright with you?" She said in an abrupt tone that was somewhat annoying but nothing I couldn't look past. Then she added "Or you could do it I mean with your extensive knowledge of robbing museums and all."

"I was fifteen and it was my first time!" I

yelled back.

"Alright dear, I was just having a little bit of fun. No reason to get your apples all mixed up." She winked back at me. "Now, while I am gone, try not to let curiosity get the best of you and stay out of that room." In order for either of us to truly hold up that deal we each took our part of the key so that we may only enter Old Merlin's door together.

As Eliza was leaving for her afternoon of recognizance, it would seem I had some research of my own to do and lucky for me, Rutland kept an extensive collection of literature in the upstairs attic. All one would need to become a master in any trade or art form. Just as soon as I hit the two hundred and eightieth step of the rather daunting staircase, and yet another un-welcomed visitor had found themselves, tapping at my front door.

I peeked through the peephole quickly only to see my cousin Holly pacing in small steps awaiting my greeting.

I opened the door slowly as it was larger than any normal door should be. "And what do I owe this pleasant surprise to?"

"Arthur, come on now don't be rude, invite your cousin in!" She said as she literally walked right past me. "So how's the new house treating you?"

"Well it's only been a few days but nothing

short of extraordinary." I found myself suspecting that wasn't her last question so I asked one of my own. "So how is the husband shopping coming along, any perspective beaus on the horizon?"

"You know how it is, tough to find one worth keeping now a days, how are things with you and Beth, You two still getting along?" She asked only making small talk.
I smiled half politely, "Sad news, Beth and I broke up."

"Oh I am so sorry to hear that Arthur!" she continued.

"Almost nine years ago…" I finished as she continued to walk through the lower level of the house with that look of, being up to no good as per usual.

"So I was thinking of having a little social gathering this evening and I was wondering…"

"You were wondering if I would go, but you see, I can't because, I am just overwhelmingly busy as it were this weekend." I cut in thinking it was a simple invite.

"Not quite!" she added. "I was thinking this would be the perfect place to host my event and since you are clearly not seeing anyone at the moment maybe I could introduce you to my friend Isabelle."

"Holly that sounds lovely it really is quite the offer but you see this weekend is just no good and Uncle Rutland wants everything left just as it is."

"Nonsense! He will never know we were even here." She walked back towards the door and swung it open. "Alright Ladies bring the decorations through here and put all drinks and food in the kitchen, the rest of the guests will be here within the next two hours."

With no time to spare, I gave out my decree to all involved with hosting this impromptu shindig. "No one is to disturb Uncle Rutland, all must stay on the main floor at all times and if anything is to go missing or damaged, well Holly would be held responsible to the fullest extent of the law." They raised their hands in agreement.

For the next five hours I buried myself in every book I could find up in the attic on Old Merlin until I came across a box of Rutland's travel journals, which turned out to be useless humdrum of pure fantasy or so I thought until I saw a drawing of King Saul's box.

The story has it that the box is literally made from the helmet of the Philistine General, that David had killed and that it contained the lock of hair Delilah had taken from Samson, and with it his power.

From the information I gathered, it would seem Merlin was trying to recreate the elixir of life before things went sideways for him and that maybe just maybe my uncle was indeed in search of the final ingredient as his dream was always immortality.

"Arthur! Arthur Sherwood!" I could hear Holly screaming for me, as the party grew louder. "Arthur there is someone here to see you!"

I pretended not to hear her as I figured she wanted me to meet Isabelle, only Holly was a persistent woman who usually found a way to embarrass me like it was her only goal in life. She poked her head up into the attic. "Arthur, some lady named Eliza is at the door for you and she said it is urgent."

"Oh right, right Eliza is here and I must see her at once. Excuse me." I said as I passed right by her and raced down the steps to meet Eliza at the door. I pulled her through the door and ran her past the gathering down the hall and into the first room I could find which unfortunately happened to be a closet.

"Well this is cozy." She uttered. "What part of normal day did you need an explanation on?"

"Yeah, about that, my cousin Holly sort of invited a few people over."

"A few!" She exclaimed. "I counted at least thirty-five people from here to the front oor. And what if one of them stumbled upon your Uncle's room?"

"I know, I know not the best timing but I

am a terrible liar and Holly would have figured something was up, so I just went with it." I deflected before bringing up the museum. "Did you devise a plan for the biggest heist of the century?"

"I did, but let's get one thing straight, no more surprises." She said as she and I awkwardly exchanged a handshake being that we were practically face-to-face given our close quarters. "Good news is it should only take about five minutes with about a six minute window to pull off the job."

"And the bad news is?" I hesitantly wondered.

"The bad news is, it's going to require two people to get the job done without a trace." She answered quickly as we could hear the party dispersing, we still needed a cover that would be normal enough to emerge from the closet undetected. Her bright idea was to untuck my shirt, mess up my hair, and let her hair down so that people would get the wrong impression and simply just keep on moving.

The closet door opened as we spilled out into the room with only Holly and a few of her friends left to clean up. "Arthur Sherwood, I would have never guessed you for a man to take a woman into a coat closet." Holly yelled out to make sure the rest of the room heard her.

"Everyone, this is Eliza. Eliza this is my

cousin Holly and her friends who were just about to leave."

Eliza cut in swiftly. "You're correct on that Holly, Arthur is not the type of man to bring a sweet woman like me into a coat closet. So, I brought him in there." She finished with a sassy tone. "Now if you all don't mind, Arthur and I have some business to attend to."

The rest of the group dissipated out the front door as Holly kept trying to linger, I could tell seeing me with a girl as stunning as Eliza, had indeed left her perplexed. The door closed leaving us in peace and quiet to plan out our next move. I started the coffee again as Eliza spread out the blue prints of the museum on the living room floor.

Chapter 2

The day arrived just shy of the opening of the exhibit; I bought one pass for the last pre-opening tour, with my only job to create a large enough distraction without legal ramifications as possible. I wandered around nervously looking on at each of the installations trying to blend in. All of my life I have lived within walking distance from this place and still this was my first trip to it. As fascinating as it all was, nothing compared to a weekend spent at Uncle Rutland's house. With ten minutes until close it was time to put my one-year of theater training to good use as I ran up to the only remaining guard on duty in quite the panic. "Sir, Come quick, I cannot find my son anywhere!"

"Well where did you last remember him with you?" he demanded immediately while adjusting his belt right beneath his lazy overhanging waistline, just as Eliza thought he would.

"Well we were coming down the second to last staircase right before the new exhibit signs, and that's the last I saw of him, it couldn't have been but only ten minutes ago."

"Alright, alright come with me, it wouldn't be the first time we had a child wander off into a new exhibit. We will have to temporarily suspend the security system from my booth in the front lobby before we enter that portion of the museum." The guard assured me that everything would be just fine.

Eliza made her way from the bathroom towards the stone, waiting for the security lights to fadeout, before making the swap.She moved through the corridors like a professional ballroom dancer with such grace and poise. She was in and out in less than five minutes upholding her end of the bargain.

Leading me into the area still being assembled, he flipped the lights on. "Well go on, call for your boy, what's his name?"

Catching me off guard I answered. "Wilson! Come on your mother is waiting for us by the car and you do not want to keep her waiting. Wilson!"

We searched for a good five minutes before Eliza finally came pounding on the front doors to the museum.

"Is there a possibility your son made it out and is the one banging on the front door?" He said as we made our way down the main corridor to investigate the noise.

He opened the door to find a very upset Eliza.

"What are you doing? Our son is past his bed time and already asleep in the car and you are holding us up from getting home. Because?" She said like any nagging wife would.

I turned to the guard in a look of help me out with this one. He seemed like a good man and indeed he would have been if I actually lost my child and Eliza was actually my nagging wife.

"Well Miss," He said. "Your husband was helping me fix one of the statues someone knocked over on the last tour, it wasn't until we tried lifting it, that we figured how long it was going to take. My apologies, for holding you two up this evening."

"No need to apologize sir," Eliza continued as I mouthed the words thank you as she was pulling me out the door. He had himself a chuckle before locking the door behind us.

"How is our son doing?" I asked sarcastically as she tipped her hat to my performance.

"He is doing just fine." As she held the

rock out in front of me, it was the smoothest stone I ever felt.

We jumped into the car with no one from the museum the wiser and drove off into the night ready to seek that which was ours to find.

Pulling down the street we noticed a rather strange sight as a glow was coming from the top window of Rutland's house. I jumped out of the car and sprinted up the steps in an athletic manner as I possibly could. Treading all three hundred and sixty five and a half steps without skipping a single one, I poked my head up into the attic door.

"Holly!!!!" I yelled in order to give her a fright as she fell out of the chair. "What are you doing up here? How did you even get in the house?"

"Oh my goodness Arthur, why would you speak at such a volume? Do you have no manners?" She quickly turned the situation around onto me.

At this point I was actually now in need of time to cool down before giving her the, this is not your house talk and you can't just sneak in whenever you want.

And breathe. "Holly, I know you are my cousin and we use to be super close but this is not a way for us to get close again. If you want to hangout or come over just call and schedule an appointment like the rest of the family."

"But Arthur, I am not like the rest of the family. Am I?"

"Well you have no definition of personal-space or gratitude which you probably got from your mother, but on the other hand you can sometimes be a pleasant encounter."

"That does it, Arthur Sherwood, I know you're up to something and if you want your space then fine but don't say I didn't warn you that this house is nothing but trouble and that Eliza girl too." She rambled as she walked down the stairs in a hurry with Eliza patiently waiting at the bottom of the step ready to greet her with a smile. She took one look at Eliza before huffing and puffing her face red all the way back to her car.

"She has some serious issues. I mean, I am no saint but that woman has a few branches loose." Eliza smiled as I nodded in agreement. We watched Holly walk to her car and pull away before merging our keys together in order to retrieve the box from behind Old Merlin's door.

We set a place mat out on the kitchen table, as we had no idea what was to come of the box once we opened it. Eliza nervously pulled the stone from her pocket.

"You ready?" She asked as I looked on unassumingly.

She set the stone in nervously as I placed

my hand upon hers and pushed it in ever so gently, until the box top flipped open and we both ducked for cover.

"Are we still alive?" She let out a sigh of relief as I picked up the note left in the box. The note had been scribed in another coded language and I mean, I am all for a good scavenger hunt but come on more coded messages which only ever lead to a riddle and another pot of coffee.

It was a good thing Eliza was here with her conveniently ready to crack the code notebook. Part of me wondered if she was just using me for the house to find her mum or if she truly cared for Rutland.

So I flat out asked her about the notebook. She then explained. "It belonged to my mother before she gave it to Rutland and I have been using the better portion of my life trying to decipher it. Some of it is just gibberish but a lot of it can be useful when dealing with salvagers. The first page alone is the Salvaging Oath which is not to be taken lightly."

It read like that of a pledge.

"I solemnly swear to take what is lost and give it back to those who have lost it, unless those who have lost it, stole it in the first place. Anything in the open sea, rivers wide or mountains deep is always the finder's keep." Signed with only their initials R.Q.S. and E.G.D.

"What do you say, we make us official and put our initials to it as well?" She looked at me intently.

"Yeah sure, Why not, let's take the pledge as we have already robbed a museum, why not add a signed confession to it." And so we did A.C.S. and E.J.D. right beneath the people we both loved dearly and missed much.

"Alright, now let's have at that letter." She said as she snatched it from my hand.

"You know you could exercise a little politeness every now and again." I corrected her.

"You are right." She said back. "I could, but I won't because that takes time and currently, time is not on our side for the usual please and thank you banter a normal partnership requires, so I move that we make all niceties simply understood without ever needing to say them. Obviously until we find the time, and then we can have ourselves a complete conversation of pleasantries."

She didn't even bother to look up from the page to address me so I simply stated reluctantly. "Fine… I second that motion, only for the sake of time but not the approval of being without proper manners."

A short while later she stood up in a fit of frustration. "I have been through every page of this blasted journal and absolutely nothing in here is relevant to this letter."

That's when it hit us both rather strikingly at the same exact moment. "The Scrolls!" We moved the painting and slid the wall out of the way, turned the key and entered back behind Old Merlin's door. We hurried over to the stack of scrolls that had been sitting on top of the box the other day. We rushed out into the living room where Rutland use to do all of his thinking and quickly unrolled each and every scroll, until we found the one we needed.

Fiercely she began to unscramble the letter leaving us with nothing more than a poem of sorts.

"With an eye in the sky,
she spread her words wide
Falling gracefully towards the floor
Every thought fleeting
as the wind still deceiving
Her companion surely fell for
And if not by day then by night they shall come
With the wave of the last call home
Should their journey begin
where the distant shores meet?
May they never forget,
the door is the key"

Giving that neither of us had ever heard these words before we had seemed to hit a dead end, which is unusual territory for such an intellect as myself to be found. "What do you say we take a break and go for a stroll around the block?" I inquired politely.

"I have an even better idea." With her hand in the air, she proclaimed proudly.

"Dare I ask?"

"I could use a freshening up and it would be more practical for me to be able to do so here. So how about you and I take a ride over to my place so I can pack a bag and move back in with you."

I pondered the notion and weighed out all of the pros and cons. "On the bright side, it would help speed up the current expedition. But the downside Uncle Rutland was specific about only me staying here. Then again."

"Then again that isn't really Rutland Quincy Sherwood in the other room anyways." She cut me off in a veracious tone. She did have a strong argument on her side of the room.

"Under two conditions. You have to leave your motor vehicle at your place so not to alarm the neighbors of any tomfoolery. Also, under no circumstances are you to interrupt my bathing rituals. I need one hour in the morning usually around 7 a.m. and about an hour at night before bed to my lonesome."

"Deal, done! I promise never to walk in on your private time. Can we go now?" She agreed.

I followed her astutely over to the place

she called home. The building was a bit dated but homely. The streets were dimly lit in the early dusk like that out of a scary story. The wind was washing through the streets as the leaves twirled towards the full moon. With the elevator currently out of service we made our voyage up six flights of steps to apartment 6E. She nervously let me enter as I could tell she wasn't use to visitors and even the most confident and beautiful of people were self-conscious of their own dwellings. Truth was, it smelled of lavender and old books, not too messy but also not white glove clean either. Her home as did Rutland's, fit her perfectly.

"So, you must read often?" I asked, trying to make small talk as I noticed we enjoyed some of the same authors.

"Yes as much as I can fit into a single sitting." She laughed, "Mother always said to be a well-read woman, is to be one prepared with purpose and power."

"I can see why Rutland was so fond of your mother." I bestowed a quick compliment to ease the sense of loss she felt while we reminisced. "Rutland told me something similar, to be a well-read man is to be one who understands a woman, and also to know when to shut up in front of her."

We both laughed as she moved all fifteen suitcases to her living room. "And that about does it."

I looked at her in a more serious manor as the current situation cut off my laughter. "And who is going to help you with all of that, did you hire a moving crew I am unaware of?"

"Oh come on, sack up, it should only take us two maybe three trips at best. Plus you could use the workout."

Two hours later we were finally packed in the car and headed back to Rutland's house, where it would seem I just couldn't escape the ever revolving door of visitors.

"Mum, Dad what a pleasant surprise?" I distracted them as Eliza made her way around back to clean up the scrolls and close the door behind the wall.

"Ah we thought you could use some supper, so I made you some stew with potatoes and your mother baked a pie for dessert." My dad and I conversed as my mum looked intently at the flowerpot full of dirt.

"Oh dear, how do you expect anything to grow when the soil is forgotten about, grab me the water hose and give the nozzle a quick turn for me." She had quite the green thumb, but I never had the heart to tell her that it was merely a pot of dirt with nothing else in it.

"Thanks Mum lets head inside to the kitchen to eat." I said nervously, before putting my hand on the doorknob as it started to turn from the other side.

Eliza stood in the doorway being charming as ever. "Mr. and Mrs. Sherwood! It is so good to finally meet you. Arthur has told me so much about you."

Mum and Dad looked stunned as Dad simply gave me a fist bump in approval as Mum let out a squeal. "Oh Arthur, you never told us you were seeing someone and surely not a woman as beautiful as she." "Mum and Dad this is Eliza my girlf…" She held her hand out with a ring on it. "Fiancé? Eliza this is my dad Brunley and my mum Pip."

"Fiancé! Fiancé! And this is the first time we are meeting her." My Mum seemed more relieved than upset.

"Well, Mum, if you must know I really like her and given your track record of scaring off any potential women in my life, well yes you now get to meet my Fiancé Eliza."

"Well done son." My dad congratulated me to cut off from any more awkward explanations that were best left for another day.My family, in particularly the women of the Sherwood's, always seem to find their nose in everything.

"Oh good you brought supper, we are starving!" Eliza continued into the kitchen with Mum to set the table.

"How long were you going to hide her

from us?" My Dad then given the chance, cornered me.

Quick on my feet I said. "As long as you planned on hiding your current job situation from Mum, I suppose." He backed off immediately.

"How is the job search coming along anyhow?" I asked to change gears as our current firm had filed for bankruptcy a month ago. "You know, entry level positions with littleto no pay but require the experience I have to be qualified for the job. The system is completely backwards these days."

"Well Dad, and I say this to you honestly because I cannot pay you yet but how about you join me in my new firm, I would even make you name partner. Sherwood and Sherwood: The Only Sure Thing in Law."

"It's brilliant but that would require telling Mum my whereabouts for the last month everyday as I kissed her off before work."

"We will tell her you were working on retaining clients for our new firm." I said reassuringly.

"Do we have clients?" he asked properly.

"Well fortunately for us we do. As I found a loophole in our firm's employee contracts which allows us under these circumstances, to take three of our top clients with us where ever we decide to go."

"Smashingly brilliant of you!"

"Here is the thing I am tied up on an important case and would need you to attend to all six of them until it is over."

"Deal!" my Dad looked relieved, like you do after a hard workout.

"Are you boys done talking shop? It is time for supper, hurry up now." Eliza called from the dining room.

"Yes, yes here we are." I entered the room as my Mum began the interrogation.

"So Eliza tells me you have made some real headway with opening your new firm?"

"Actually I have made a little too much progress, so with that I think it would be bestfor business if Dad joins me. Now, I know he will make a little less than he currently is making to start but being a name partner has its benefits." My Mum sat up intently as my dad began to explain the situation.

"Pip, it will be perfect, yes my salary will go down a bit but we can finally take vacations when we so desire and the good news is, whatever we bring to the table is ours to keep. No more hoping the bonuses will be honest every year, and no more working on Christmas."

"That sounds delightful, and it is good news too because Steve called the other day to see how you were doing with the firm filing for bankruptcy." My Mum always found out the truth because like I said, nose in everything.

"Oh Pip! I' am." My dad began to apologize.

"I know you are and I knew that if you didn't find something soon, you would be moving in here with Arthur." She laughed.

"So Eliza, what do you do for work?" My dad quickly changed subjects.

"I am a nurse by day, and a nurse by night." She quipped.

"And have you and Arthur set a date for the wedding?" My Mum continued on without letting us breathe to enjoy the meal.

"I myself would love a summer wedding but your son Arthur thinks a winter wedding is just what we need." Eliza was spectacular at keeping up appearances.

"Oh, that is my Arthur, always enjoyed the winter season. Never the weather however, only the season brought him true pleasure. Can we be expecting to meet your parents before the big day?"

"Well, my Dad died when I was younger and my mother left me about ten years ago, so unfortunately it will just be me." I thought the night would never end and that is when my dad stepped in just in time to call it an evening.

"This has been quite lovely and Eliza you are everything we could have asked for our son and more. Pip are you ready to go dear?"

"What is the hurry Brunley? We have only been here a few hours?" My mum tried to convince him to stay but my dad stayed the course insisting he had some work to get done for the new firm in the morning and that they can set up another time to come over notifying me at least a day in advance.

We walked them towards the door as to make sure my Mum did not linger as it was another quality that ran in my family and unfortunately not one I was a fan of.

"Drive safe, love you guys and Dad I will call you tomorrow with an updated client list, feel free to work from home until we can find a more permanent place."

The door closed as Eliza let out a sigh of relief pulling her apron off and tossing it back into the kitchen. "If I had to play Susie Home-maker for even another minute, I may have snapped." She exhaled. "And one more thing, now that we are engaged, which was brilliant by the way because now we can ask your mum and Holly to plan the wedding for us which will in turn keep the unwanted lingerers out of our hair."

I looked at her in a peculiar expression. "Who are you? No, really are you a spy, am I helping you with a top secret mission, how do you just get into character like that at the drop of a hat?"

"Growing up I played loads of chess which mother always said would come in handy, when getting into the family business. You play?"

"I fancy a game now and again."

"Perfect!" She answered challenging me to a game. "This will help us take our minds off the current puzzle and sometimes when you focus on a new problem. The answer to an old one rises to the surface of your thoughts."
And so it had begun, a grueling match of pure intellect verses pure instinct. She may have played a few more matches in her lifetime but chess is merely tracking patterns and reacting to variables as they come your way. She stood up as she put me in check, I arose as I knew the final move was coming, I gave the board one final look from above as she never saw it coming. I slid my final piece in giving her nowhere to go. "Checkmate!"

"Well played Arthur!" she put her hand out in a sign of good gamesmanship, so I spun her around and took her for a dip, as we both needed a good laugh. I am not sure what I did wrong as she ran off really quickly and returning in that same moment with an idea on how to solve the scrolls.

"Here help me, lay them out in numerical order then come with me." I could see her mind moving at rate that she need not stop to explain her process but to simply go along with it.

"What are we doing at the second floor over look of the living room?" I asked hesitantly.

"It occurred to me that when you spun me around for that dashing dip of a dance move, that maybe we were looking at the scrolls all wrong, right side up, we can't seem to make heads or tails of it but what if you were to hold me upside down?"

With her back against the banister, she pulled me uncomfortably close, before she sat on the railing of the overlook. "Do you trust me Arthur?"

I gulped before nodding. She wrapped her legs around my waist rather tightly; while using my body as sort of an anchor she slowly bent backwards. "Hold steady, Arthur hold steady!"

At this point I could feel sweat dripping across my forehead. She then began to draw what she saw, which escalated the pressure on my hips even more than before, I thought my back was surely going to snap at any moment.

"Almost done!" She announced before snapping back up nearly head butting me to the floor. She winked at me before stealing a kiss, which she said was for good luck as she ran down the steps like I use to on Christmas morning.

"Um excuse me, would you mind explaining to me your sudden change in neuron productivity?"

"It's an inverted pictoform! My mother used to do these with me all the time as a child which means, she is alive." We embraced as she cried happy tears; it was the first moment of humanity I saw in her since she came blazing into my life three short days ago.

"That's superb news but how do we get to her? And is Rutland with her?" I asked gently.

"Those scrolls were dated just two weeks ago, if my calculations were right and that means that she somehow got a message to Rutland and I am guessing it was an S.O.S of sorts that would give plenty of reason for him to leave unannounced. Now whether or not he got to her is completely up to fate."

Being a lawyer for as long as I have, I could tell that she was withholding some sensitive information but it was not time to pry. We simply enjoyed the victory that her mum and Rutland were somewhere out there in another time and another place, alive, in desperate need of help but alive.

"If that is all for tonight, I think I am going to head off to my pre bed bathing ritual." I told her in confidence, which was the first and only lie I ever told to Eliza.

I went upstairs, I just suspected her of not just knowing where to find her mum and Rutland but my gut told me she knows how to get to them and is waiting to venture off on her own.

I put on a pair of boots, trousers and a button down shirt worthy of all the great adventurers of our time. Loaded up my knapsack and waited for her to make her move. I wasn't much for a stake out as I dozed off frequently only to be startled by the sound of the wall shifting. I slowly made my way towards the steps as I heard Old Merlin's door being unhinged.

"And just where do you think you're going?" I gave her quite the fright as she stood there with a bow and arrow holstered and a hooded cloak as if she was ready for a battle of such. "And what on earth are you wearing?"

"Look Arthur if my mother is alive, I am going to find her and you cannot stop me and it isn't worth it for both of us to go, who knows what may be waiting for us on the other side."

"I appreciate your concern, but you are not going alone, haven't you gone at this life alone enough? Look, I may not be much in the department of brute strength but I am quick on my feet and I dare you to challenge anyone to match my exceedingly high level of intellect." I said making my case that she didn't get a vote in either way.

"I am going with you, and that settles it."

She looked on in awe. "And where has this man been this entire time, such confidence, such fervor. Now, let's get going before we have anymore unwanted interruptions."

She cleared a path to the carved stone in the middle of the room and grabbed the two swords off of the wall.

"Here take this and on my go, we are going to strike the stone at the same time."

"And what exactly will that do?" I asked genuinely concerned with her lack of explanations.

"If everything goes as I hope, well we should be transported by chance to where ever it is your uncle and my mother may have been last." She replied earnestly but not completely honest.

"Alright then let's give it a go." I approved.

The blade's cold steel struck the edge of the stone causing an eruption of energy followed by a vortex of light, and like that we were gone. It was like a great void had been crossed in an instant and yet somehow I could still hear a familiar voice that wasn't Eliza's.

"Arthur! Eliza? Is anyone home? Your mother asked me to stop by to get some ideas for the wedding." Holly was calling out to us from the other side and then her voice was gone. I couldn't remember anything in that moment. "Arthur, are you home?"

Holly walked into the room where the false wall had come unhinged from the recent events that had occurred. "Arthur! Come out here right now." She demanded as she pushed the wall back giving way to Old Merlin's Door, which we unfortunately forgot to close behind us. She made her way past the threshold with caution as her eyes widened to the sight of everything the room contained. She walked to the furthest wall picking up one of our swords along the way for protection. Spooked by the shadows beyond the book cases she ran back towards the door tripping over a stack of rusted armor, she fell towards the edge of the stone, striking it with the very sword that would send her into the same void, Eliza and myself had just crossed. Our worlds would soon collide.

Chapter 3

The daze wore off as we found our bearings just inside a tree lined bank leading to the forest's edge. A cool wind whipped between the branches and right over our heads. Footsteps marching along a near path grew louder as Eliza quickly covered us behind one of the largest trees I had ever seen in my life, that was when the horn sounded, and we realized that we were trapped in the middle of a battlefield.

"Stay down, I will come back for you." She said pulling an arrow from her quill.

"O yeah sure not a problem, whatever you say?" I mumbled to myself as an axe struck the tree behind us. That didn't stop Eliza from running straight into the fire.

She took down three men twice her size in the matter of seconds. "Come on we need to move, now."

We ran as fast as we could deeper in the woods away from the two feuding sides only to be cut off by the shadows that ascended from the treetops. We were surrounded by a group of what seemed like a hundred men at the time.

"Drop your weapon and remove your hood!" Declared a stern voice coming from the large hooded figure that stepped out from the ranks. "What is your business in the Shadoway Forest? Clearly you are not a part of the Knights of Agnar? But surely wanderers in these parts cannot be up to any good!"

Eliza replied in a language so regal that it could only be that of royalty. "Elowas ke-lend t'uvieste. No'mek le-wan'd j'eswin." The group of soldiers surrounding us lowered their weapons and kneeled before us.

"Are you seeing this Eliza?" I held to her.

"Arise Keeper!" Eliza spoke with authority.

The cloaked figure removed his hood,

"Forgive me queen but I was unaware of your return."

"Finlay! Is that anyway to greet your oldest friend?" Eliza removed her hood.

"Eliza? When did you get back and who is this lad you strung along with?"

The two embraced as I awkwardly waived to the rest of the group kneeling on the ground, "Hello, I am Arthur, Eliza's newest friend you all can find your footing as well and if by chance has anyone of you seen my Uncle Rutland around?"

"Sorry but we don't know anyone by that calling." Finlay quickly answered. "This is Fergus he is as strong as a Drak'on and as big as a… well clearly you can see for yourself his behemoth stature." I reached out my hand hoping he would not crush it in one fell swoop.

"This is Lachlan and his brother Muir, they can make a boat out of just about anything." The two stood side by side as I could see them measuring me up before they bowed to Eliza once again.

Both had piercing green eyes and full ginger beards with dingy long hair.

"Please, to meet you both." I nodded.

"Next we have Duncan, who can handle anything with a blade and never misses a target. Once he sets his sight in on it, well they are as good as dead." He put out his knife handle as a sign of respect, his skin was a caramel and his eyes were stone cold hazel as if they were calculating the distance between every object in the forest at once. His senses peaked before he flung his knife behind his head and into the chest of one of the surviving enemies that they had just thwarted in battle rendering him no longer alive as he tried to escape.

"His family has hunted in these woods for generations." Finlay continued seemingly un-fazed by the blood spatter that had just landed on his shoulder.

Eliza and I looked at each other, I more so horrified than she. "Dually noted!"

"And last but not least this is Rory and though he be smaller in stature, there is no tree or rock that he cannot climb. And as you are Eliza, he is fierce with a bow and arrow. We are the last remaining Keepers of the Lost Kingdom of Findas"

"It is good to meet you all but I must see my mother right away." Eliza said before Finlay pulled her aside.

"Your mother has been taken captive by a group of scavengers upon the order of King Ag-nar that he would slaughter every village from here to the River of Dagrun to the Hills of Halle and all the way out to the cliffs by the Sea of Idunn, only until she surrender herself and so without haste she did for the sake of her people.

We sent our greatest tracker to run them down and report back with her whereabouts."

"Um excuse me, would you mind sharing with the rest of us." I nosed my way into their conversation even though it wasn't a particular trait I was fond of in other people.

"Look, Arthur, my mother was taken captive sending her soldiers to retreat deeply into the Shadoway Forest." She turned back towards Finlay. "Can you take us back to the camp? We must rest up and prepare ourselves for a rescue mission."

We made our way through the dense woods as night began to fall. The group moved with such precision I often found myself in trouble of keeping up. Breathing heavily. "You think you should have mentioned the whole princess thing or maybe that you, I don't know, are a first class archer with no qualms for taking another's life."

As we continued swiftly she explained. "First of all no one has called me princess as I have been a long way from royalty in quite some time. So, please forgive me for lack of formalities and second of all you only assumed that I couldn't handle myself in a fight. Which, you're welcome for saving your life back there."

"Are Rutland and your mother even partners in the salvaging business?"

"So to speak, best not to worry about it

now. I am sure they could explain it a bit better than I."

I decided to drop the topic for now as we came up to what looked like a dead end with each member of the group one by one disappearing into the trunk of the tree ahead of us. "Come on!" Finlay grabbed onto us both and before we could even say a word, we were into the camp.

"Welcome to Eve'les Cieler Tho'n a refuge for anyone escaping the peril of King Agnar."

A boy who appeared to know Finlay well, "Daddy you're home", approached us! He jumped up into his arms as if he hadn't seen him in a long while.

"Arne! Look how big you got my boy. It's only been like three months and I swear you are another foot taller." Finlay exuded with pure joy.

"Actually it has been five months and eight days, but who has been counting." A woman's voice called approaching.

"My dearest Althia, Oh how I have missed you." They held on to one another for a fair bit of time before he introduced us. "Althia I want you to meet Eliza daughter of Queen Evelyn and her friend Arthur who have travelled far in search of a man they call Rutland."

"Oh your majesty it is an honor to meet you, please forgive my humble appearance and

I am sorry but we have no one who goes by that calling you seek, here with us. Also by all means call me Thia."

As the greetings winded down Finlay gave order. "Duncan, I need you to go at once and tell the Elders we must hold counsel tonight. Rory, see to it that the night watchers are on high alert for any sign of scavengers near camp."

We were given a very brief tour of the camp. It was quite a sophisticated venture they had going on here. You had your farmers keeping up with some crops in one end and hunters carving up their kills of the day in the other end.

The builders seemed to be working around the clock to keep up with the demands for new dwellings. They literally have survived here without any connection to the Inner lands for years.

"And this is where you two will be spending your sleeps." Finlay pointed us through the doorway to the dwelling.

We dropped our bags off as Duncan returned with news of the Elders being ready for counsel.

In a sign of respect, Finlay kneeled before entering the tent for counsel as he gave Eliza and myself a royal introduction.

The Elders taken back by her return

bowed in solidarity before moving to embrace her one by one, giving her a kiss on the forehead honoring her mother.

"You have your mother's spirit, I can see it in your soul." The last elder greeted her.

"You may all be seated and as the Last of the Royal bloodline, I now commence this counsel into session. Finlay the floor is yours." Eliza found her seat in her mother's thrown.

He moved to the center of the room. "Agnar's forces are growing stronger every day and every day we lose more ground waiting for Vadimas to return from the Sea of Idunn." He turned back to the elders. "So I, along with the permission of the Elder counsel and the help of the Princess, will lead the Keepers of Findas on a rescue mission to save the Queen."

"And what about the prophecy?" The second of the elders exclaimed, she had this grandmother like quality to her demeanor.

The head elder stood up in a solemn state. His eyes could tell an infinite tale and his wrinkles would only be further proof of the wisdom he gained throughout his life. "Before even the galaxies had a chance to shine, there was a prophecy of a time such as this, which the fallen kingdom will rise on the eleventh day of the eighth sun bringing new life to all the inhabitance. And should the sun fall before the restoration of the ninth moon, eternal darkness shall forever be."

I interjected nervously as I only wanted to find Rutland and given the tone of the elder's statements, I had some questions. "Hi, yeah, excuse me, pardon my lack of procedural knowledge but what day is it currently?" I moved towards the center of the room.

"It is the third day of the eighth sun, of course!" The head Elder spoke wisely.

"Oh yes of course silly me, that gives us less than a week to figure out how to complete the restoration of the ninth moon and what does this process entail."

"It is said that a man from beyond the stars will reign down in completing the royal trinity causing the moon and sun to part ways and restore balance to the Lost Kingdom of Findas and in doing so ending the reign of Agnar's terror."

Eliza spoke next, "It will not do well to dwell on what we cannot change as the man beyond the stars is but a wish for now. So, let us find food and rest, and tomorrow at first light we can devise a plan to rescue my mother and restore the ninth moon."

The counsel dispersed as Eliza and I retreated to the dwelling prepared for her return. It was as elegant as one could make it considering the location and lack of resources, with a few added touches as I set up a makeshift desk for critical thinking as I believe one must always have a designated area to ponder, no matter where they find themselves in any moment.

"So did you know all along? Or did you hit your head hard enough to remember as we transcended both time and space which I for one am completely still trying to grasp." I asked her directly.   "Arthur, come here, have a seat." She moved towards the edge of the bed like structure.

"O yeah, it's story time, finally!" I let out sarcastically.

"About ten years ago, my mother did go missing but it wasn't because she was lost it was because they were trying to protect me. But five years before that my father was murdered by a ravenous scavenger king whom they call Agnar. The people of Findas went into hiding."

"And how does Rutland fit into all of this?" I let her continue.

"Your uncle and my mother went in search for a sun dial built by Sol and Mani soon after the first war. It has been said to be only legend but it is the key to the restoration of the ninth moon and completion of the royal trinity."

"I assume that he came here often then. Do you know if they found it?"

"Your uncle has been coming to Findas for quite some time bringing all sorts of trinkets and goods as he was a very knowledgeable man, my father and rightful king of this land called your uncle to be his only royal advisor in matters of enlightenment and merriment which often one led to the other. One, day when our people were in hiding, Agnar set out a decree and put a bounty on the royal bloodline, that we were to be killed on sight if found and so my mother sent me away with Rutland. Unfortunately the dial was never found before he had to leave. I was ten years old when he brought me to London and in order to keep me safe I remained hidden from his family and friends studying every day to learn more of your time as well as training for my return to Findas."

"That is not possible, I was over Rutland's house often as a child and no way could he have kept you a secret that long."

"Not possible? After all the impossible things I just told you, you truly believe that keeping me from you and your otherwise dysfunctional family was impossible for Rutland."

She figured I would need convincing. "Remember the night you slept over his house because your parents went away on holiday and you asked to sleep downstairs because you thought a monster was in the attic?"

"I do, I was most certain of it and still to this day I haven't been able to figure out the mystery." Foolish me didn't connect what she was saying until she stood up and spelled it out for me.

"It was me you goof, I was the one making all of the noise, not on purpose but Rutland had forgot to mention he had an overnight visitor. I was trying to send a message to my mother when I fell off the chair. As soon as I hit the ground I heard you scream for Rutland and thought the jig was up. I froze in place for the better part of two hours."

"You know I still check closets and the attic for unwanted visitors because of you."

"Sorry?" She shrugged. "Anyway the next day Rutland figured I was old enough to live on my own and bought me the apartment across town, set me up with an allowance to live off of and encouraged me to embrace life as a Londoner. As he feared my mother had shut down all communications with the right heart as Agnar would stop at nothing to destroy every last part of Findas, including me."

Arne interrupted us at the doorway.

"Pardon me your majesty and Mr. Arthur. The feast is ready and awaits your blessings."

"We will be right out Arne, thank you." Eliza said to give us a moment, as he bowed out of the doorway.

She looked back at me. "Let's finish this conversation another time. The people await us."

We walked towards the center of the camp where a fire was blazing and cheer was all around. Word had spread that the princess had returned and all were invited in a celebration of sorts. We were greeted with wreath necklaces and glasses of wine made fresh that morning. The music of the people was a sound of hope that they hadn't had in a very long time.

Eliza stood before the crowd and gave out the blessing. "Fes'tave tun pore'las!" The crowd cheered as the food filled the tables around the fire. With Duncan to my left "Arthur can you pass me the plate of Hobblegils?"

Unsure of what he was referring to, I began to point until he gave me a nod of approval. I leaned back towards Eliza, "And what are Hobblegils exactly?"

She informed me that it was like a turkey but not really as it found its place in the sky. Duncan again asked, "Arthur, can you pass me the Hornedsplat spread, please?"

I again leaned into Eliza and again she informed me that it is a type of jam from one of the fruits that grow wild in the forest. We feasted for hours as the dancing and music continued. For us we had only been there but a day but I couldn't imagine what it must be like for these people who lived in fear for so long and now have a glimpse of hope in the form of a princess and her less than adequate highly intelligible right hand man.

Sitting on a log by the fire as I watched one after one come up to Eliza bearing gifts of gratitude. I was then approached by one of the elders of the tribe; she walked with a cane and slight limp in her step, carrying what appeared to be a necklace of sorts.

"Give me your hand my dear." She said with a gentle whisper. I thought she was going to do something magical, like tell me my destiny, I spaced out.

"Well are you going to help an old lady to her seat or not." She said needing help balancing as she sat down. "Ok dear let us have a good look."

"Excuse me? But a look at what?" I said curiously. "Is Eliza playing some sort of funny on me?"

"Your eyes, give me your eyes. The eyes of a person tell you more than just what they have seen but also in the right light what they truly hope to become."

"Alright, let's give it a go." I almost soon regretted that statement. She started to hum softly, then swiped a red streak of paint across my forehead all the while wafting incense around us. Our eyes locked in the burning embers of the fire and I could feel her pulling on my soul.

"Ahh, interesting, very peculiar." She said. "Not

quite what I expected but we can make this work."

"What! What is it?" I looked to Eliza for some help but she just gave me, the look of, you're on your own.

"Patience!" She held up her hand. "You are a man of good value, one who upholds the needs of others even if it is putting your desires aside but some times that means you miss out on the true joys this life has tried to send your way. It would also seem, you have quite the affection for Princess Eliza."

"That was a little broad, don't you think?" I questioned her method.

"You think you're better than your family and have worked so hard to distance yourself from them, that you don't actually enjoy what you have become. Your cousin Holly, is it? Needs you now more than ever. You were close once and all she ever wants is to be close again, she doesn't have anyone she can talk to like you two use to."

The last part was a little more specific then I would care to admit, actually there was no logical explanation as to how she would know who Holly was and on that note. "Eliza? Are you ready for bed, I mean sleep?"

"It is getting rather late and we will have to be up by first light." She yawned in agreement.

As the night grew deeper and the noises stranger, sleep seemed to slip away from my grasp. I thought about a time when Holly and I started a food fight at the family Christmas dinner and then the time we broke, well I broke my parents' kitchen window, but she took the heat for it because she at that point could do no wrong in the eyes of our family. As the memories continued to storm my mind, I slowly faded to the dark clouds of dreamland.

"Rise and shine you, it is time to begin your training while Eliza and Finlay make headway on finding the queen."

Duncan tossed me an apple like edible object for breakfast that was sweet to the taste and perfect to the texture.

Duncan was designated to me in effort to make sure I wouldn't die at my own lack of skills. I wasn't going to be completely useless as I have had a few years of fencing under my belt, that along with a few rope-tying courses at university, they still had their work cut out for them.

"First thing is first, let's find you a suitable weapon."

The axe was too heavy, the first sword was too long, I wasn't a good shot with an arrow and all of the shields were slightly too big.

"Um do you have anything smaller or

lighter maybe something I could throw?" I inquired as I had quite the arm as the star bowler on my town cricket team.

Duncan replied by simply showing me the throwing knives from the inside of his jacket like over coat.

"Now you are talking my language." I said excitedly.

He set up targets at different ranges, and angles as he put it. "Enemies will come at you without a second thought and you must be fully prepared. On my go neutralize the threat."

I began to take them out one by one as I ran through the field of targets, feeling high and mighty I let out a sort of mocking laugh. "Is this all you got?" I turned and faced him slowly as he threw a blade right past my face and over the rock behind me directly into another target. "You missed one and if this was an actual real battle you would be dead or worse you could have got one of your own killed. Now I am going to set them up again and this time try not to get one of us killed."

"Yeah but it was just a piece of wood really, can't do much damage now can it?"

"Right you are Arthur, so on this go, I will be throwing knives at you to give it more of a real life battle scenario."

"Are you joking right now?"

He smirked holding up multiple daggers

in one hand. "Good luck and God Speed!"

I gulped as he wasn't joking with me and before he said go the first dagger flew right at me nearly clipping my ear right off.

"That's just a flesh wound, only but a little nick! Could you imagine if it was to the heart?" He laughed as we trained for the next three hours of target practice before moving into hand-to-hand combat, which Duncan was sort of the expert on.

"Now that we have figure out your skill set we must find the right harness to hold your knives and give you the freedom to defend yourself in a close quarter combat." He had me try on a few different models before I found one that I could make work with a few added alterations of my own.

"Rule 1: strike with precision or do not strike at all. This will help you conserve energy and keep focus." He then demonstrated with precision as he put it.

"Rule 2: sometimes defense is your best offense. Allow your opponent to put themselves into a position that favors you by directing their steps and using their momentum." He then continued the lesson by throwing me over his hip and applying pressure to my shoulder as my face was pressed against the cool soil of the forest floor.

As I was down there he decided to go over

the last rule. "And Rule 3: never under any circumstance allow, no strike that, rather give up the advantage and always finish the job."

"Agreed." I said wincing in pain. "Could you let go of my arm? As it has started to lose all ability to feel."

"Oh yeah, sure not a problem, I am sure if you ask politely one of the Knights of Agnar will surely let you go free." Duncan said sarcastically as I began to calculate the possibilities. Using what little energy I had left I slipped the rock out from under his footing, rolling through to a higher position, I removed his own dagger from his belt and placed the blade into the ground next to him. "Let me go!" I declared with heaviness in my breath.

"Well done Arthur, well done." Duncan congratulated me as I tipped over towards the ground purely exhausted. He then gave me help up as we went down to the creek to wash up before returning to the camp.

The Keepers gathered with Eliza and Finlay as I sat in the background simply ease dropping on the plan to return the queen to safety.

It seemed the spy sent out to track down the queen, came back with troubling news as the scavengers had split up the convoy on their way to King Agnar with a second prisoner in tow.

Their voices escalated. "Look, with Vadimas still out to sea, we simply do not have enough trained Keepers to go after both crew of scavengers." Finlay stated.

"But if we go after the wrong one then my mother is as good as dead." Eliza seemingly frustrated. "We cannot afford any mishaps."

"What if I told you, you're both right and wrong?" Rory interceded. "It is true we are down a man but we have something we never had before?"

"What madness are you speaking of? I am pretty sure we have nothing new here." Finlay pressed him for an answer.

Rory leaned in and nodded in my direction. "We have an outsider with us, who is to say he doesn't fit the bill as a wanderer, whom surely could hide in plain sight, with no one the wiser."

I was informed later that a wanderer was a free person who pledges allegiance to neither kingdom. They were also left to fend for themselves as long as they do not steal or cause harm to the land or its inhabitants.

They all turned to me in one big stare as Eliza began to draw up the plan. "Finlay and I, along with Lachlan, Muir and Rory can head off the group heading along the river's pass. Duncan, Fergus and Arthur!"

"I beg your pardon, what possibly could I be of use for in such a mission?" I found myself in the awkward predicament.

Duncan pulling me aside, "Well you see, Eliza has informed us of your ability to entertain and while you distract the driver of the cart heading toward the High Cliffs, Fergus is going to bull rush it tipping it while I take out any immediate threats and hopefully we save the queen if not we rescue the other person being held captive by those scum."

"Ah, yes why that sounds simple enough. This should be a jolly good time." I said nervously as though I had a choice.

"Perfect it is settled then. We will leave within the afternoon to begin tracking and we will make up the ground lost, at night. From what we know they travel for three hours at a time resting for five or even longer. This should give us just enough time to cut them off before they reach the Inner Lands which will be swarming with the Knights of Agnar." Eliza dismissed us to ready ourselves for the missions.

There is a theory I have about being unsure or unready. Prepare as much as you can for whatever you can and when you feel your preparation has run out, let instinct take over.

Chapter 4

With six days left until the restoration of the ninth moon, myself, Duncan and Fergus set out towards the High Cliffs near the Sea of Idunn. I was humdrum with all kinds of folly, as I wasn't completely settled with my current whereabouts. Last week, I was a lawyer in London, England trying to venture off into my own business and now I was literally living inside one of Rutland's extremely maybe not so anymore tall tales. With Eliza and company heading to the river pass with hopes of rescuing the queen, we moved ever so quickly. We hoped to cover enough ground to cut off the scavengers before the next nightfall, in our quest of reclaiming the land of the lost kingdom.

"So about how long did you say it would take until we reach the High Cliffs?" I asked as Fergus answered in a deep mellow voice.

"About one solar change, if we can keep a good pace up, we may be able to head them off even sooner."

"You know, we have a queen where I am from but I must say I have never seen more loyal servants in all my years. Do you really think our plan will work?"

"It is a bit of a dodgy plan isn't it?" Duncan added that we had the advantage of them not expecting us. So they would be taking proper rests along the way. I have seen many places in my few trips abroad, but I have never witnessed an endless blue sky blazing with the heat of two suns.

"There is only one sun actually, here have some water before you go mad." Duncan tossed me one of the wine skins filled with water. "We should find some shade up ahead to rest for a moment."

By my calculations we had been at it for a few hours and if we wished to make it by next nightfall, I would need to budget our rest time wisely as we have no way of knowing truly how much ground we had to cover. We broke our bread sparingly and sipped our water even more so.

"So what's it like?" Duncan asked. "Where

you are from Arthur?"

"Currently I live in a country that has been surrounded by war for the better half of a decade, much like Findas we are people rich with tradition. We enjoy our food much and our drinks even greater."

"Do you have a lot of family?" he continued. "A wife? Offspring?"

"I do indeed have a large family in number but rather not close in relation to how you live here. And no wife or children; for love has not been my fondest hour."

"That's a shame, Eliza seems to really like you," he smirked at me.

"How about you Duncan? How did you meet Finlay and the rest of the Keepers of Findas?"

"Fergus, Finlay and myself have known one another since birth. Our parents were all great friends and from day one they knew we would be too. I still remember the first time Fergus took on a Drak'on with his bare hands and well as you know he is still alive so."

"What is a Drak'on exactly?" I asked nervously.

"It is the only thing above us on the food chain, would be wise not to cross paths with one. It has the face and fangs of a Saber tooth tiger with black scaly skin like that of a serpent, runs like a cheetah and breaths a gas that if it

so choices can torch the surrounding area in an instant annihilating everything
in its path. The average size of this beasty is about two and a half Fergus's."

"Right yeah ok, note to self, see a Drak'on and run away." I laughed.

"No never run, hold your ground and stair it directly in the eyes. Do it right and one of two things will happen. It will either bow in a sign of respect of your fearlessness in which you may hop on and it becomes your spirit animal or it will eventually attack you anyways and in that case by all means run." Duncan finished talking of the monster with a smack on the shoulder.

"After we lost our parents in the first war of the sixth sun, we grew inseparable. On that day we made an oath to protect what little land we had left at all cost knowing that soon a time would come for us to reclaim that which has been lost."

Fergus' eyes watered up as he put his fist up to his chest in a sign of solidarity with Duncan. This world was soon revealing itself to not be so different from the one I left behind. We continued our journey onward with one goal in mind, to bring home the queen.

The road ever winding and cliffs within our site we decided to go off the marked roads and into the wilderness. Part of me did as fearfully as I was more than happy to still know I had a sense of intuition but then this overwhelming sense of adventure took over my mind and I decided to lead the way throughout the night.

We could hear the waves crashing in the distance as a soft rain fell upon the ground washing away any tracks we may have left behind but also making it near impossible to keep up with the tracks of the scavengers.

"Alright let's rest under the trees up ahead until we catch a break from the rain." Duncan took a glance at the map he had folded up in his pocket. "If I have a good read on this they should only be about two hours ahead of us, given that they start setting up camp two hours before night fall we should be able get to them at the second cliff."

"Perfect." I saw a proper lead in and ran with it. "You think the other crew is doing alright I mean with well tracking on a river can be quite difficult." I only assumed it would be as my dad use to take me fishing every summer on the family boat, it was quite tedious work.

Duncan reassuringly said, "They are more than fine, with Lachlan and Muir at the helm, those two have been on water before they could even swim. Not to mention they have explored just about every body of water Findas has to offer. If they had it their way, they would live out at sea but unfortunately Agnar has taken hold of even the water villages where they grew up."

The rain started to let up as we strapped ourselves back up, I carrying all the necessities, as I was to look like a weary traveler when the time was right.

The first cliff approaching was the most important of our passes, as we needed to go undetected.

"Fergus, you keep a look out as I get Arthur across and then when I signal, you follow up behind." Duncan pulled me along swiftly before signaling to Fergus.

"Well that seemed easy enough…" I claimed before turning around stepping right into a…

"Arthur, look out!" Duncan yelled pushing me out of the way as he was trapped by what only could be described as bigger version of a bear trap.

It was quite a contraption and once it had its captive, it was wise for the person to stay completely still. That was when a man holding a spear emerged out from the rock wall he was completely blended into, holding a spear pointed directly at me.

"What are two Keepers of Findas doing near the High Cliffs with a wanderer?" the man demanded.

"We are on a mission to rescue the Queen

of Findas!" I said promptly.

"She was taken by a group of scavengers on the orders of King Agnar."

"Is that so Wanderer?" he questioned my validity.

"Yes and well you see the princess and I..." He cut me off.

"The princess has returned? Are you sure of it?" he continued to doubt.

Duncan completely stressed out trying to not let the spikes get any closer to his neck stuttered. "it, it, its true Eliza herself has returned."

The man released the trap taking a closer look at Duncan, "Duncan is that really you."

Duncan stepping out of the trap and turning around to face the spear wielding man. "Hachiro? It is so good to see you my old friend!"

"Did she find the man from beyond the stars?" Hachiro spoke like that of a general.

"I am afraid not but she said to tell the tribes of the Outer Lands to prepare for battle." He held out his hand in a manner of greeting.

"Akemi!" Hachiro yelled suddenly as another figure stepped out from the rock in which they were hidden in. "Go at once and tell father that the princess has returned, it is time to ready the troops and take the war to Agnar."

Fergus looked at Akemi in all of her beauty as he tried not to let us notice he was blushing. I was onto him even if no one else recognized the way those two looked at each other.

"So you say you need help rescuing the queen, got room for one more?" Hachiro was well built, and one who seemed to me like a valuable asset to the mission as he knew the high cliffs frontwards and backwards.

"I will have to talk it over with the group..." I joked before realizing he was lacking a sense of humor. "Of course we have room for one more, please lead the way actually as we must make up for some lost time. I am Arthur by the way."

He found us a shortcut through the very road we thought to go around, putting us in a perfect position for an ambush rescue.
We waited patiently for two entire hours before we saw the scavengers approaching, maybe a few more than expected but nonetheless I stumbled out into the middle of the road pretending to be drunk.

"Move you wandering scum!" The driver of what appeared to be a horse drawn carriage being pulled by human like beasties.

As soon as it came to a complete stop, I gave the signal. "Now who do you think you are calling scum, you rat trap of a scoundrel."

I bent down to remove the dagger from my ankle holster slinging it into the face of the driver as Fergus came bouldering in knocking the cart off its wheels. Duncan and Hachiro took out the remaining scavengers counting three kabobed on his spear alone and four currently sporting daggers to the heart. Fergus ripped the door off the cart as I found myself staring at the impossible, no improbable is more like it.

"Holly! How in the? Never mind that, are you ok?" I asked knowing it was more than likely she was about to read me the riot act.

"Am I ok? I don't know I just spent the last few days in the back of this cart being slobbered over by those mongrels."

"So, you'll live?" I couldn't resist a quick jab to lighten the mood.

"Uggggh! You are simply intolerable." She pushed right past me before bumping into Duncan who knocked her off her feet.

"Oh forgive me Queen." He said before realizing. "You are not the queen!" He offered her a hand up and it was the first time since we were kids that I could remember Holly being without words.

"I am afraid not, and you are?" Holly said bashfully.

"I am Duncan, madame, are you a friend of Arthur's?"

"Oh yes, I am Arthur's cousin Holly, it is getting quite hot here would you say?" She said before fainting. We moved quickly back to the first high cliff where Hachiro offered us a place to stay the night.

Hachiro's tribe kept hidden between the rocks like that of the forest people of the Shadoway. Duncan found Holly a place to rest and some new clothes; Akemi even brought her a pair of shoes to help with the traveling.

"Oh these are quite comfy, did you make them yourself?" Holly inquired of the shoes.

"My mother made them out of castacus fur, each pair is handmade, let's just make sure they fit for travel." Akemi put her through a variety of quick tests to make sure the fit was right, as the rest of us were to see the head of the tribe.

Hachiro's father and loyal servant of Findas, who at the time of peace; was one of four chieftains' in the land of Findas. He was responsible for the High Cliffs and protecting the land from any intruders trying to use the Idunn overpass to gain entry to Findas. He was a man of honor and he stood just short of my chin, with thick eyebrows and long mustache. He moved with wisdom as he allowed us to enter his chamber. "My son with whom I am pleased, tell me do you have news of the Queen?" his father held his arms upward for embrace as Hachiro was a few inches taller than me.

"No sir, but we are confident that Princess Eliza and the other Keepers have rescued her properly. We will only know for sure when we set back for the Shadoway camp in the morning."

"Ahh, quite right you are to have confidence as there has never been such an air of hope in almost a decade, your sister told me the princess had returned and in doing so I sent word to the rest of the tribal leaders. If the prophecy were said to be complete within the eleventh day of the eighth sun; then it would be wise for us to prepare ourselves for war. The tiny squalls and mini battles will simply not do at this hour."

"Aye sir, we shall ready the soldiers at once and move them to the Inner Lands' borders at dawn."

"I don't mean to pry but it would seem that Agnar has quite the army at his command numbered in the thousands of well-trained ready to die for him at a moment's notice. We simply can't show up with a posy of villagers." I interjected.

"Forgive me father, this is Arthur friend of Eliza and ally to the Keepers of Findas, you may have known his Uncle Rutland who he believes was an advisor to the King."

"It is ok son, we must not apologize for the excitement of an outsider. That is true what you say of Agnar's Army but understand this, the people of Findas are many and their hearts all in." He pulled me aside. "Rutland you say your uncle is? I haven't seen him since the fifth sun or was it the eighth moon? Either way an odd fellow he was but a good man and if you share his blood then I say welcome to the Village of the High Cliffs, whatever you need simply ask."

Hachiro, showed us our way to the hammock like structures we would be resting in, the stars were out shining as the breeze came in off the sea, we laid up under the crashing waves.

"Do you think the man from beyond the stars will show up soon?" Duncan asked.

"I hope as much as I can and if not I will stand my ground until death or eternal darkness." Hachiro answered.

"Just curious?" I asked. "Does anyone know what this man even looks like?"

"He is said to be a wanderer of sorts, he is the one to complete the royal trinity, bringing restoration to the lost kingdom."

"Well that certainly doesn't narrow it down." I muttered.

"It doesn't have to narrow it down for you to believe he is real. Haven't you believed in something you couldn't see?"

Duncan asked genuinely concerned of my doubts.

"I mean you for instance, you mysteriously show up in the middle of the woods with the princess days before the prophecy is to be fulfilled in a land you never knew before. I don't question that and yet you hear the words from beyond the stars, yet still doubt it possible for a man to travel from that far."

Holly being nestled under Duncan's arm also chimed in. "Arthur has always been a man of numbers, facts, and realities leaving him shortsighted to all possibilities."

"That is sort of true I suppose, but one cannot truly live with their head in the clouds all day."

"For being Rutland's favorite it would seem he didn't wear off on you much, don't you remember all of his stories of his adventures to the world in the stars?"

"Holly, what did you say?"

"You were Rutland's favorite?" she said as if I was upset with her.

"No, no about his stories."

"Oh, those, whenever I would visit he use to tell me stories of a place just like this."

"Oh really?" I said sarcastically.

"Yes, really, you weren't always Rutland's favorite you know. Actually, I was rather jealous when you became his golden child."

"Is that why we grew apart?" I asked knowing it was true no matter how she responded.

"I guess, I just wanted to be the one to go

on adventures with him when I was good and ready, but he chose you the paper pusher, and yes I pushed you away."

"Oh, Holly, I had no idea that was the case. I wish you would have said something sooner."

"Yeah, well, let's put it behind us because we both did stuff we regret and should forgive the other one right."

To be honest, I had done nothing except tolerate her irrational behavior for so long but in a sense I guess she was right, if we were ever to make it back home, we would need to put any quarrels behind us.

"Yeah, sounds like a good deal, Holly. Now how about the stories Rutland would tell you did he ever mention the royal trinity or anything about the restoration of the ninth moon?"

"All I remember was he spoke of a beautiful queen and her daughter, it was as if he truly knew them. The last story he ever told me was in hopes that one day the princess would return to the lost kingdom and reclaim the thrown from an evil king."

"Did he say how?"
"He only said that the answers she needs lie within her heart."

"Another riddle? Why couldn't Rutland just spell it out?"

I found few thoughts laying there in my hammock, which was quite comfortable I might add, as I drifted into a short lived sleep. Word of the princess' return spread so quickly through the kingdom that it caught the very edge of Agnar's ear that he sent out troops in the middle of the night to scour the Outer Lands. I awoke to Hachiro's hand over my mouth to keep quite as some of Agnar's spies were just beyond the road leading into the cliffs.

"We must go at once, to meet up with the others but quietly as to not be detected. The Keepers of the High Cliffs will take care of the spies." Hachiro ordered as we followed holding sacred to our breaths to make our travel more speedily his father released to us his favorite horses.

"If you come with, then who will order the soldiers preparing for the war?" I whispered.

"Akemi will lead them into battle as she has lead them many times before." He answered quickly. "My only job is to make sure you get back to the Shadoway safely. Now less talk and more walk."

We rode in formation for the next hour until there were no signs of the spies. Breathing heavily Holly let out, "Can we take a moment to catch our thoughts?"

"Let's make it to the edge of the forest

before we rest." Duncan assured her, she could ride with him the rest of the way but Holly being competitive as she was wouldn't have it. As we came to the edge of the wooded pass, we were greeted by a hoard of Agnar's most barbaric warriors.

Fergus grabbed all the reigns and tethered the horses behind the thickest tree he could find before placing Holly properly behind the barricade of the same exact tree. That is when Duncan and I took on the first of five assailants. Hachiro was quite handy with his spear like staff as he went straight after the biggest one in the pack.   Then there was Fergus who in what seemed like one gigantic punch, knocked out the remaining attackers. "Is that all, you got." He yelled. As three of them scurried away, one still out cold, while another was out permanently.

"Let's pull this one out of the path before we are seen." Hachiro suggested as I tended to Holly.

"Are you alright, I mean, how are you? I feel like I haven't asked you how you are in a really long time."

"I have had better days my dear Arthur but as much as this has not been my finest hour it certainly is not my worst either." We walked side by side with my arm around her as if we were kids wandering the yard in search of Rutland's lost treasure on Easter Sunday that was until Duncan gave me the sign that he wanted to cut in. Given that he was not only an honorable man but also Holly needed him more than me right now, as they seemed to be hitting it off smashingly.

"Put me down you swine!" our visitor thought it was best to kick and scream as Fergus placed his face firmly into the ground.

"Now listen you, if you don't give me the information I need, this will be your last sunrise." Hachiro said placing his spear on the back of his neck.

"You fool. You think death is my biggest fear? You truly underestimate Agnar's abilities." He scoffed at us.

"Well then I guess you will not be needing this." The scream echoed far enough surely for even Agnar himself to hear it, as Hachiro's blade went through the tips of the man's fingers.

"Hachiro, what are you doing?" I grabbed his shoulder before he struck again; instead he removed his upper garment with all scars on display. It was unlikely anyone would fully recover from what we just saw.

"This pestilent pawn thinks I don't know what Agnar is capable of, I have some bad news for you. Not only do I know, I also gave Agnar a scar or two in the process. So I am going to ask you a question and you will answer it."

"Just kill me now please."

"There will be time for that later." We sat him up and wrapped up his hand. "Now tell me what you know about the restoration of the ninth moon."

"Look, all I know is that it can only occur when the royal bloodline has returned to Findas." He spat out.

"Returned? But the queen never left." Duncan added in.

"Even though the Queen never left it is her daughter who is the key, for she carries her father's blood within her body and is the only remaining heir to the thrown of Findas. Only she can dethrone Agnar. Well, at least that's what we were told when we were sent out to kill her."

"Well this has been a revelation but I am sorry, this is where we leave you." Hachiro stood up and with a quick motion released the man's soul into eternity. After a brief readjustment and quick cover up, we then headed to a far more direct root back to camp hidden far in the Shadoway forest to wait for the Queen's return.

Chapter 5

The night grew older as the fire dimmed, still no sign of the other Keepers. Finlay's wife Thia joined us, as she also could not find the strength to sleep until their return was certain. One of the people of the tribe began to play a mandolin softly as the most majestic of songs was being sung in accompaniment.

"Thia?" I asked politely. "What was Findas like before Agnar's Reign?"

She gazed into the flame. "I was but a little girl of the time you speak of. The land was full of life and the people love. The fields grew with such vibrant colors. The crops were plenty. We had a trade port open at all times of day from the most northern shore to the south side lakes. Findas was a place of opportunity, tradesman would come from all over just for a chance to be able to stay, to start a life most only dream of."

"Sounds magical."

"It was. But those days are far behind us now."

"Yes but soon, soon those same days will be ahead of us and then with us. I remember every morning getting up bright and early with your father to head down to the market for all the freshest ingredients in order to keep up with the bakery orders." The older woman from the other night sat down by Thia at the fire. She looked across at the outsider whom she knew not of but spoke to anyway. "You must be Holly, come here dear let's have a look."

"I beg your pardon, but a look at what?" Holly hesitantly stood up, gave a glance back at me.

"Go on Holly, let her have a look." I nudged her along and told her to trust me.

"You have to be joking." She muffled.

"Ah yes, eyes of green, longing for adventure, self-sufficient you are, but then why feel the need for another to complete." She hummed some more, as Holly looked on.

"Arthur, what exactly is going on here?"

"Let her do her thing, I promise you will be fine. It will only hurt a little." I joked. And like that it was over, only Holly looked stunned as if everything the old lady said was completely true. As I stood up and looked past her I saw a wounded Lachlan being carried in by Finlay and Muir followed by Eliza who looked like she had been through hell.

"Quick, bring him to the healing tent at once." Thia grabbed Holly who had some basic first aid training.

"We need to seal up the wound as quickly as we remove the blade which had been broken off at the handle." Holly grabbed an iron press and rushed towards the fire putting it in at its hottest point.

"Finlay and Muir, you are going to need to hold him down for this next part." she stuffed a piece of cloth into his mouth and told him to bite down. He was struggling to fight back the scream as it muffled into the cloth, Althia pulled the blade out, and she quickly poured cool water from the untouched creek with in the forest, cleansing the wound, as Holly pressed the flat iron fresh out of the fire onto the wound sealing it. Muir wept and moaned for the better part of the next two hours as we tried to get to the very bottom of it all.

"Eliza, Where is Rory?" Duncan demanded as she began to tearfully tell the others.

"We had just made it to the river's end when we came upon the scavengers. Only Agnar's men were tracking them as well. As we took down the cart and the first two scavengers, we were ambushed." She held her hand over her mouth. "Rory didn't make it his body was cast out to sea by the river's run."

I approached her and held her tightly. "It is not your fault, come on, it is going to be alright."

"And what about the queen?" Hachiro asked intently.

His question was met by a familiar voice. "The queen has been taken to the inner lands, far beyond the castle walls. My intel has told me that she is alive still, but for what purpose of Agnars' is certainly unclear."

Duncan ran over to him blocking my view. "Vadimas! Your back, it has been far too long brother. You must come and sit, we have so much to do and not so much time to do it in."

He brought him over to the common area as we waited for Lachlan to awaken. "Of course you know Fergus and the rest of the Keepers and now Princess Eliza."

"Your majesty." He bowed with a wink before turning to us.

"And now this is Arthur and his cousin Holly all the way from their home in London." Duncan finished as we ran towards the one they called Vadimas.

"Uncle Rutland, you are alive and well." We embraced for he was his sprightly self with a little more toil on his body than usual.

"Oh my dear Arthur and Holly you made it." He squeezed us both tightly as if he never thought seeing us again was possible. "It is just so good to see the both of you. I wanted to come back for some time now but the way home was closed."

Even though his beard was a little fuller and his stench a little muskier, his smile was as kind as ever and I now fully understand in this moment more than ever why he asked me to refer to him as the Incredible Rutland Quincy Sherwood, because it was true. Though I was quite happy to find him alive, part of me still was upset with him for more than just a few simple mishaps.

"Did you by chance get my message, the one I left in the will for you alone?" He quickly asked as soon as we got a moment to ourselves.

"I did." I answered knowing his next question was to be.

"Well did you bring it lad?"

"One moment please." As I went diving into my knapsack looking for the bottle of ink he strangely requested. "Here you go, the container of ink from your writing desk and I thought you might also want your pocket watch. It hasn't worked since we have been here but for old time sake I figure you would enjoy a comfort from home."

"You have always been one for detail." Before he could tell me I was his favorite in the family, I had an obligation to ask him about Holly.

"And what about Holly, why did you push her away and take me under your wing."

"Understand, Arthur, I never meant to hurt her. It is just that the prophecy always spoke of a man from beyond the stars and I just thought that if it could be anybody it would be you."

"Do you realize how insane that sounds? And on top of it all, you left Holly heartbroken not to mention her and I lost a lot of time together because of it. You made her resent me for what? A prophecy in some magical land no one from our world has heard of."

"Look, you have every right to be mad at me Arthur but it wasn't until I realized that the man wasn't you, it was too late. I was stuck here with no way of telling you." He said apologetically.

"And Eliza, got an explanation for her to?" I continued.

"I couldn't tell anyone of Eliza's true identity, they would have locked me away in the loony bin and tossed out the key."

"Holly would have believed you, I would have even given you the chance to explain. Instead all I got was an irrational fear of closets and attics, thank you very much."

We bickered for the better half of an hour until he brought up sort of a truce. "We can argue about this until one of us runs out of air and simply keels over or we can get back to the group and figure out how we can stop this world from complete oblivion. Because if you die here, then there is, no you there."

"Please excuse me for a moment." I said bringing Holly back to Rutland as I made him apologize. "Holly I believe, Uncle Rutland would like to say something to you."

"Oh alright, Holly I am sorry that I ignored you when you needed Arthur most and I am sorry that it almost cost you two your friendship."

This was the first time in a long time we three felt like a real family should. The moment however evaded us quickly, as Eliza summoned us to the war room, as I liked to call it. Honestly, it was a tent with a table, some maps and tools of sorts all predicated upon the battlefield.

"Agnar may out number us in theory but if we hit him from multiple sides, it would highly favor us in the end." Finlay started in on the logistics we would face. "Also, there is the matter of the restoration of the ninth moon."

"The only way we can complete the restoration of the ninth moon is from inside the castle, and unfortunately the only person who can restore it is that of Royal Blood." Rutland spoke solemnly.

"No! there has to be another way, we must not put Eliza in anymore danger." Finlay was up in arms on the matter as we were still unsure of whether or not the queen was alive.

"I hear what you're saying but even if we win the war, Findas will be left to eternal darkness when the prophecy goes unfulfilled."

"So we will live by fire's light."

"I will not abandon my people to the darkness." Eliza spoke up. "We will infiltrate the castle take down Agnar and restore Findas to its rightful ruler, my mother Queen Evelyn."

The debate continued as Hachiro sent word to Akemi who was wading on the border of the Inner Lands ready for war. The letter read, "Akemi, it is time to hit Agnar with every soldier we have. We must not take his army head on but from all sides. It is the only way to defeat such numbers. Fight well, and live honorably. With all of my love, your brother Hachiro."

"Eliza, Arthur this is what we are looking for." Rutland drew what was only to be a replica of Old Merlin's door.

"Old Merlin's door, have you lost your mind?" I questioned his method.

"No, no that is something I never had, but yes you see Merlin made a second door and I put it in the castle as a favor to the king and queen for times such as this. The door is meant for safe keeping and that of keeping things safe."

"And where is it precisely?"

"Here comes the tricky part. It is in the throne room as the king always wanted an eye on it at all times."

"Oh yes right, probably right where Agnar will be waiting for us." I yelled in frustration.

Eliza looked up at me as the rest just looked on into the impossible. "Maybe that is not a bad thing after all, as you must know of the saying two birds one stone."

"Speaking of things that come in two, there is also the matter of unlocking Old Merlin's door. The key was split in half, one I know for sure one part is with the Queen Evelyn, and the other however is rumored to be buried with the king's treasure in the caves of Idunn."

"This is lovely, we are on the brink of war with a plan that you ask me is pure fantasy and now we are off on a treasure hunt." Finlay and Hachiro seemed less than pleased with our current predicament.   "Well if there is one thing I do know is this, Rutland can find just about anything he puts his mind to and the rest usually finds him. So Eliza myself and Holly will accompany Rutland to the caves of Idunn in search of one half of the key, while the rest of the Keepers and Hachiro save the queen we can meet back by the Western Falls tree line. As that is the closest point to where the queen is being held."

Duncan added. "As soon as we rendezvous to merge the key, we should only send back in those who need sending."

"So you myself, Rutland and Holly will make sure that Princess Eliza makes her way to the throne room."

Holly looked up, "Why me?"

"Because our only way home may be just beyond Old Merlin's Door."

"Brilliant Arthur." Rutland smiled.

"Who is with me?" Eliza asked, as the room grew quiet.

Duncan stood up with his blades in hand. "Even if in death or eternal darkness, I will always be with you."

"In three days should the sun not rise, we will burn a fire brighter than that of a thousand suns, and finish the battle we have started." Finlay raised his sword knowing he was leading the rest of the Keepers into the heart of the war.

One by one we pledged our allegiance to that of the lost kingdom of Findas, before partaking in a hopefully not last meal ceremony of sorts.

The soldiers prepared to take leave in the night as Rutland and myself made sure we had everything we needed for our journey to the North Port. We said our farewells as I overheard Duncan and Holly in deep conversation.

Duncan siting on the forest floor, with a peculiar book open in hand, Holly inquired. "What is weighing on you, Duncan?"

"Just finding solace in reading from the Book of the First Days."
"Would you read some to me?" she sat right beside him.

"The stars must receive him until the time comes for the Keeper of Keepers to restore everything, as he promised long ago through his prophets. He will restore the royal bloodline as in the days of old. Afterward you will be called the City of Hope. A place for all to be at peace with one another." Duncan looked up to see Holly intently listening. "After two days he will revive us; on the third day he will restore us that we may live in his presence. The Blàth na Saol will bloom as a reminder that he is with us."

"Blàth na Saol?" Holly inquired.

"It is the flower of life." Finlay cut in the conversation as he passed by. "Not a single soul has ever seen one since the first light of Findas. Who is to say even then that they didn't make the entire story up?"

"Someday Finlay you will take comfort in the unknown and faith in the unseen." Duncan said lovingly.

"Just look around you, clearly he has abandoned us. It would be wise not to waste any more time praying for a miracle." As Finlay continued on his way to be with his family I found my moment to take part in their lovely conversation as a man of higher learning, I always make sure to indulge my soul as much as my mind, even if I believe there is a rational explanation for the seemingly unexplainable events of old.

"And just who is it that Finlay speaks so bereft of belief in?"

"He is said to be the maker of Findas and all of its inhabitants as well as the lands of the north and as far to the east, as one can travel before the point of no return. It is believed that on the First Light he gave way to the seas and forged land by his own hand. Still, not enough he made creatures for the air to ride the winds and clouds, for the sea to balance the waves and for the land to uphold all of its provision. On the second day of light he created the likes of man and from there a woman so that the man would not be alone. He charged them with taking dominion over the world he created leaving them to be fruitful in all their endeavors. On the third day of light he made his home amongst the stars, where it is to be understood that he will bring restoration in a time of war, only when the seventh royal trinity is complete. He is the man beyond the stars as it was also told in the prophecy." "And how does this rare Flower of Life factor into all of this?"

"As he shaped the Hills of Halle and carved out the High Cliffs he made way to the very center of the land flowing with new life and from the barren soil sprouted a single flower, lined with royal red tips, and a soul sort of blue when in full bloom. It was the only soil in all of the land that was to go untouched. As the flower was a reminder of his presence."

"What happened to it?" Holly asked as if she truly believed every word Duncan breathed.

"It was destroyed in the first war this land had ever fell victim too, all seemed lost in the days that followed. As on that day the Keeper of Keepers returned to the stars permanently. This led to Findas' first anointed ruler as well as the banishment of those who caused such a travesty. It is believed that they sailed over into the place of no return." He spoke so vividly of the first days that I found myself believing him as well, only I may have still looked at him like he was out of his tree on this one.

"You know Arthur you don't have to believe me, but it would be wise for you to start believing in something more than just your own perspective for a change, if you truly wish to make it home to where ever it is you stumbled out of."

"Even there I fear my dear Duncan, I only believe in that which I can calculate."

"Ah yes a man of your mind surely can calculate yourself a way back home then." Duncan excused himself to finish out his time of meditation while Holly and I were left to our own conclusions.

"You know Arthur, you don't always have to be right, and no one person could possibly have predicted our current state of events!"

"Yes, understood. But then if this so called creator truly loved his creation, why would he do nothing within his power to stop the wars, end the senseless killing and bring peace to all the people, his people."

"I ask that same question myself every week in church, but sometimes though the answers you need aren't always the ones you hope to find." We moved on quickly as it was not a topic that would bear us any good with our newly discovered need to find the other of half Old Merlin's second key. We saddled up the horses gifted to us by Hachiro's father right as Lachlan came running behind.

"Hold up!!!" He yelled running out of breath. "If you are to go undetected at the North Port of Idunn, you will need a guide, I will be best to serve in this capacity as I am unable to lift my arm let alone hold a sword."

He saddled up with Holly who has been riding since she could walk. With the sun setting behind us beginning the first of the last three solar changes before the ninth moon was to be restored, we road with haste on the path marked out for us though it was the one less traveled.

Chapter 6

We took cover beneath the stars as we could hear the clanging of swords and shields for miles. The wind was roaring furiously as the night grew thin leaving us just enough headway to find the first of two landmarks we were to pass on our way to the North Port. We stopped off to find our faithful steeds some food and water as we continued on with rationing out more portions of a fruit like chewy substance that nourishes you rightfully so.

"Rutland?" Eliza asked as we were with fewer ears to hear and she was in need of procuring some sensitive answers. "How did my parents truly lose control of this kingdom?"

"As far back as I can remember it was right after the sixth war of this age, that ships from a far off more desolate land came piling in with people by the droves. Being the compassionate souls your parents were, they allowed all who needed refuge to find rest here, it was never to be a permanent solution but a sort of kind gesture in time of need. One man saw it as weakness, Agnar soon infiltrated the castle in need of work claiming asylum here. He just bid his time until all his men were in place. That was the day your father went to find himself among the stars."

"What kind of low life would dare use ones compassion against them?"

"It is believed that Agnar is from a royal line of his own, his ancestors were the ones cast away in the First Days to the point of no return. Though at the time it was said that one shouted from the horizon. 'One day your kingdom shall fall at the hands of the banished ones!'"

"If it is revenge he seeks, then surely he will find it at the end of my arrow."

"That's the spirit." I gave her a nod of approval.

"And what if we cannot complete what

we set out to do?" Rutland tried not to detract from the conversation as Eliza was in sort of a moment on her own. "Killing Agnar will only bring you momentary satisfaction, but it won't make a difference if eternal darkness claims this world."

She snapped back out of her heroic moment and back into reality. "This life is but a fleeting series of moments…"

Rutland bringing the conversation to a peaceful stopping point. "And if the moment should present itself, by all means take the shot but let's keep focused on the items of priority here."

"So it is settled, restoring peace to Findas and getting us home is right above killing Agnar, everyone please take note." I could see that Eliza was seemingly frustrated.

"Come on now, have at it." I pulled her aside as Holly and Rutland attended to Lachlan's wound.

"You know I always dreamed of the day I would meet Agnar, what I would do if I had the chance. But Rutland is completely right and if I am to be queen one day I must be able to put the people of Findas above even my own needs."

"Look, let's do what we need to do now and worry about you becoming a queen later." She seemed relief as we prepared our horses to finish the last leg of our journey before making the rest of it on foot. The Hills of Halle could be seen with ease against the starry sky. It was quite the view if not for the eerie drone of death all around us.

"Quick, up ahead there is an old abandon dwelling we can tie the horses up at as we make the rest of our trek on foot." Lachlan slurred, as his conditioned seemed to worsen.
"Are you alright, you don't look too well?" Rutland asked as we pulled up to the dwelling.

"I am fiiii…" He couldn't get the words out of his mouth before falling off the horse rendering himself unconscious.

"Perfect, without him we are as good as dead."

"Not necessarily my dear boy!" Rutland said while rummaging through some of Lachlan's things pulling out an old map he kept on him for times of comfort. "Here is the perfect way of entry into the North Port, there is a dock that will lead us to the underwater caves where hopefully we will find the funeral ship of the late king as it is said to have been sunk before ever leaving port."

We prepared ourselves for the waters, as it would seem not all of our gear should be submerged into the depths of the Idunn. "Holly, you must stay here and make sure Lachlan is out of site ok? If he is to awake, you must keep him quiet."

"We will be back before you know it!" Eliza reassured her.

With diving socks gifted to us by Lachlan's bag of all things needed to survive on water, we made our way down to the port, which was being watched over currently, by two underwhelming guards.

Eliza being ever so shifty decided to run in like a damsel in distress claiming she had been attacked by one of the Keepers of the Lost Kingdom.

"Take us to him immediately." They demanded as she led them away, Rutland and I came up from behind and took them out quite handedly as it were, moving them onto a smaller boat and pushing it out into the current. We then located the dock with the missing floorboard as it was there as a breadcrumb for all who knew of the caves below.

"We may be the first people to ever set foot down here since the day your father went under. Just prepare yourself for what we might find."

"Well said Rutland, let's give it a go." I nervously jumped in the water as the sun was coming upon the horizon, followed by Eliza and Rutland.

"Take three deep breathes in and exhale on the last one you will hold and follow my lead as it will be a good forty-five second swim until we reach the caves."

We swam quickly and with near flawless execution if I were to say so myself or at least the best we could. We resurfaced to that of a light sitting on the edge of a table. "Well it would seem we were not the first people here since your father, well you know. Hopefully the key is still here. Shall we begin our search?"

The candle came in handy as we found a lantern in need of lighting, it was clear that someone else was on the trail for the same object we were in need of. We dug through every last piece of wreckage before the ground started to rumble with a violent hemorrhage of power, dislodging the casket from its shallow grave. Rutland and I pulled it up and onto a slab of unused rock so that we could further investigate.

"I know this isn't what you had in mind when being reunited with your father but I fear we must open the casket in order to obtain the key."

"Do it immediately before another serge happens."

"3-2-1…" The casket opened as I turned away from it Rutland let out shocking noise.

"The king is gone!"

"Like just a skeleton gone or completely disappeared kind of gone?" I asked presumptuously.

"Gone! Gone! Like that time you wanted to play hide and seek and you couldn't find me for almost two days kind of gone."

Rutland scanned over the casket in search of a last chance kind of hope and he ran his hand along the fine carved wood, as the ground began to shake again he yelled at us to head back to the surface.

"No Rutland, we won't leave you!" Eliza said.

"Arthur, get her out of here now." He screamed like I never heard before. I grabbed her hand and headed back to the surface where we waited for what felt like an eternity with no sign of Rutland.

His hand plunged out of the water and onto the dock as we pulled him up ever so urgently, he had the key in hand. Lucky for us the king and queen spent some time with Rutland as the key was found inside of a hidden compartment with in the casket.

As we made it to the top of the road leading back to the abandon dwelling we turned around to see the dock being completely submerged in the water.

"Come on, come on you have to hold on Lachlan!" Holly spoke in a loud whisper as we came upon them. His wound was reopened and she was covered in his blood as she tried to save him.

"Holly I don't think I am going to make it. It seems this warrior has swung his last sword. Please make sure that it wasn't in vain, tell Eliza she must defeat Agnar. Findas must rise from the ashes once more." The blade of the sword caused a massive swelling at the sight of impact until it burst infecting his vessels. "I did everything I could." She cried as it was the first time she ever had someone die in her arms, Lachlan slowly faded towards the light.

"Here, here." Eliza walked her outside. Rutland and I moved Lachlan into a place where we could bury him with rocks and say a little prayer. We rounded up the horses as we were getting ready to make our way back to the Western Falls tree line but something had them especially spooked. So much so that mine unfortunately ran off down the road.

"Drak'on!" Rutland mouthed loudly pointing over to the horses as mine escaped. Unfortunately for us it would seem that this might be the end. As they hid inside the dwelling in hopes that the beastie would just scatter off, I decided that we had only one choice.

There was no running as the Drak'on was not one to give up on its prey as soon as it locked its senses in on us I knew it was time. I stepped outside and walked over to the road and picked up a rock, thinking the entire way over that I myself was a complete loon. I then tossed the rock at the Drak'on to get its attention.

There I was, I could see their terrified faces looking through a window way as I stared right into the soul of the beastie. Its breath was foul with a stench of rotting flesh. Its skin was black as the night, its teeth as sharp as any sword I ever saw and it was indeed the size of two Fergus'. At first we did sort of a dance I stepped; it stepped, I never once unlocked eyes with it. Since one of two things was about to happen I figured it would be best for me to position myself at the edge of the small embankment. It closed the gap fast as I dove out of the way it lost its footing on the rocks and fell right down the slope being pinned between two boulders that tumbled after it.

"Arthur!!!" Holly Screamed as she ran over to me in a panic.

"WELL DONE LAD!" Rutland walked up to me at the edge of the incline in a sort of slow applause.

"Don't you ever do that again, you had us all worried." Holly hugged me for a quick moment.

"Always full of surprises you are!" Eliza jested.

"Waaaaaaaaaaaooooorlllllll" The Drak'on let out a cry as it was in quite a bit of pain; I felt it pulling on my spirit.

I started towards the path directly to the injured beastie. "Arthur, what on earth are you doing?" Holly yelled.

"We can't just leave it there to suffer." I begged of them. "Can't you see it will die if we don't go down there? We must help it get free. I only wanted to buy us enough time to escape, not kill the creature."

I knelt down by its side as it was breathing heavily. I placed my hand the top of its head as I could see nothing but pain in its eyes its scales warm to the touch and smooth like velvet. "There, there everything is going to be alright."

I turned to Rutland. "Help me move this boulder."

"Are you mad?" He quarreled.

"If this works then I will be a genius." I crouched behind the boulder and began to push as I felt a hand on top of mine; it was that of Eliza. The Drak'on staggered up to its feet before gaining its ground again and tensing up in a position to strike. I pulled Eliza behind me and made my way slowly over towards the creature, I looked it dead in the eyes with my hand out as it bowed to wards the ground. I mounted it as Rutland gasped from afar. I put my hand out to Eliza. "Well are you getting on or what?"

"You truly are mental aren't you?" Holly let out from the top of the incline.

We road throughout the day as the horses tried their best to keep pace with my newly acquired certainly unconventional friend.

There was a gentleness to its stride and calmness as I got on. It was a moment that would not be soon forgot, as I am sure the Keepers will be beside themselves seeing me roll up on one of the most feared predators in all of Findas.

We pulled off the side of the road as we found ourselves at a temporary camp set up to care for soldiers being wounded in battle. The ground was red from the blood lost but the morale was high as not all of it was from the armies of Findas.

The crowds looked onward in amazement as we made our way to the overseer of the camp. He was said to be a magic man of sorts. "From the line of Merlin no doubt." Rutland started in on the very day he met the first in the line of Merlin's.

"I was on an expedition to a place not so far from our homeland when I stumbled upon his magic shop. There wasn't a potion in the world he couldn't brew; now what those little concoctions were capable of was up to the one who took the potion. I being one for curiosity picked up a potion that wasn't quite balanced yet, and poof it exploded right in my hand leaving but a single scar from the glass bottle breaking. So if this truly is one of his relatives it would be best not to touch anything."

"Understood, let's just take a breather gain our footing and continue our way to the Western Falls tree line." Eliza reminded us of the main goal. So with that we stayed a few brief moments and loaded up with some essentials for the next two days it would be crucial for no mishaps to occur.   The man known as Merlis approached us, "Your, Majesty. The reports are in, that Agnar's troops have wiped out the entire army sent to the western border of the Inner Lands and that currently his troops were moving towards the south."

"No time to worry. We must be on our way now." Eliza said with a straight face, as she feared the worst had happened to her mother and the Keepers.

"Please take this, you will know what to do with it when the time is right." He handed her a little cloth like bag and we were on our way with high hopes for better days.

Chapter 7

The current of the Western Falls was crashing to the river's bed like thunder in a storm filled sky; we were waiting for the rest of the Keepers at the edge of the war. There was devastation for as far as the eyes could see, fire ravaged what was left of the battle fields keeping a day light shine into the early dusk. My heart had grown bounds in the last days as did my imagination, things that seemed so important to me lost their appeal as my priorities seem to shift in a more people oriented direction. I saddled onto my Drak'on and waited at a look out point as the others caught some shut eye for a little while.

"How about we give you a name?" I said to the beastie as it nodded in excitement. "Perseus, a name fit for such the regal creature you are." He seemed to take quite nicely to it.

It seemed like forever until I finally saw some sign of life coming up the horizon. "Kaw-kaw, Kaw-kaw!" I signaled to the others as Eliza joined me in anticipation of seeing her mum.

"Do you think she is really with them?" Eliza was hopeful.

"Those Keepers would either find her or die trying and by die trying, I mean they will take out everyone in their path to do so." Rutland joined us.

The distance grew closer between us as the figures were now on a direct path to us. "Quickly everyone get behind Perseus!"

"I'm sorry who?" Holly held out her hand.

"The Drak'on Holly, the bloody Drak'on!"

"Oh no need to get your knickers in a bunch Arthur!"

"Would you two cut it out before I cut you both out?" Rutland smacked us both on the back of the heads. "Nothing like, old times, aye!"

"Queen, get behind us!" Hachiro and Finlay quickly raised their swords towards Perseus.

"STOP!!!" I ran between Perseus and the Keepers.

"Arthur, what are you doing, have you

completely lost your leaves?" Finlay yelled.

"No you don't understand this Drak'on, well my Drak'on Perseus is on our side."

"What in the great name of Findas are spewing on about?" Duncan step forward.

"Well we were coming back from the port when he came out of nowhere, so I did what you told me, I stood my ground."

"You are a lunatic, a madman. I was only joking."

"I could have died and you were just playing around."

"But you actually managed to tame the beastie."

"Well sort of, once I had his eyes locked with mine, he took a lunge at me. Pinned by a boulder I couldn't just leave him to die. It was when we lifted the boulder that I gave a good long hard look into its soul. It bowed."

"And you just got on like you were mounting a horse?"

"I hate to break up this little story time of sorts, but where is my daughter?" Queen Evelyn removed her head covering as the sun hid behind her angelic silhouette. She was definitely Eliza's mother, those eyes I could recognize anywhere.

Eliza stepped out from behind Perseus and ran over to the queen as the two of them held on to the memories.

"I have counted the stars every night for your return."

"Oh mum, I have missed you every sunrise." As tough as these women are, I sensed an overwhelming feeling of joy to the point of tears.

"You have your father's nose but everything else is mine. Oh my dear I just can't believe I am actually holding you."

"Maybe let's save the small talk and reminiscing for a more permanent time?" Rutland cut in.

"Rutland, you are as handsome as ever. I am sure you took quite adequate care of my Eliza?"

"He did indeed, So much so his own family did not know of her existence until a few days or so ago." I introduced myself. "I am…"

"You must be Arthur, your uncle has told me quite a bit about you." The Queen went on. "And who is this lovely woman with you?"

"That's his cousin Holly!" Duncan ran over to her as if they had been in love the entire time.

"I can see someone has taken a fancy to her!" The Queen made Holly blush.

"Your majesty we must not wait any longer." Hachiro warned us of the ever-escaping time conundrum. "Plus the longer we wait, the less of a chance Darsus will have making it out alive."

"Darsus? The wash boy from the castle Darsus?"

"Yes the one and the same, I wouldn't be alive if it wasn't for him. We cannot leave him behind." The Queen demanded.

"Pardon me your majesty, we received word from Akemi that they need reinforcements on the northern front." Finlay said dimming the conversation to the reality of the war.

"Take this!" The Queen held out her crown that had been split apart. "Take it to the lower Hills of Halle and tell the Chieftain that the royal trinity will be complete before the restoration of the ninth moon."

"Why do we need the crown?" Hachiro asked.

"Because an old friend once told me." The queen looked back to Rutland, "Always have a dove in your pocket!"

Which is the equivalent to having an ace up your sleeve. Rutland spoke up. "After the land stood divided and the tribes of Findas went into hiding. We thought it be best to cut off all communications until the time was right. She split her crown into four pieces to present as an offering of protection if any of the leaders of the tribes were to receive another part of it, they would not be able to turn down the request of the messenger."

"Now take this and use the Great Eden Pass to move troops from the Hills to the western front."

"The western front? But there is no war on the western front?"

"Exactly once we reclaim the castle! We can use it to take down Agnar and his armies from within. We have to force him to fight on all fronts."

"It's worth a shot, I hope!" Finlay, Fergus, Hachiro and the rest of the remaining Keepers set out for the battle field as Duncan set out to the lower Hills of Halle.

"Come on lets have it!" I asked the Queen for the other half of the key as Rutland pulled out the part we found in the underwater tomb just below the north ports.

The Queen unraveled her hair as the key was currently being used to hold up her tightly wrapped bun. "Here you go, hopefully it still works after all these years."

Eliza held up one end as I held up the other we moved back off the path, just in case it did anything magical. The key merged with a certain shine to it. Eliza tucked it away under her wrist wrap as the Queen spoke quickly about the occupants of the castle.

"The western gate is currently unguarded as they feel they completely won the western front. Once inside the walls we must find our way to the first staircase which will more than likely have a guard on it every five minutes." She continued moving her hand along the wall line. "As soon as we make it to the second level we must move quickly towards the throne room, which will be the last door on the left."

"And what shall we do with Perseus?"

"Leave him at the gate to thwart off and distract any unwanted company!"

"That settles it then, on we go. By my calculations we are heading in to the final solar change before the restoration of the ninth moon is to be complete." Rutland held out his broken pocket watch.

The path to the castle was laden with the atrocities of war but for what cost is there, that one should lay their own life down for? Freedom was the simple answer, the only answer really, whether they find it in this life or the next.

"So what do you think of Arthur?" I overheard Eliza ask her mum about me.

"He is quite fit, a little on the lighter side of things, but from what Rutland tells me he is quite the thinker which is a good quality in a man, no doubt."

"And Rutland and you are just friends?"

"Come on now Eliza, best not to pry into the past and just let it stay where I left it."

"Oh alright but I do think he would be

quite good for you!"

"So Holly what do you think of Findas?" The Queen brilliantly shifted gears to take our minds off of what certain dangers may lie up ahead.

"It is quite beautiful, never seen anything like it in all my life."

"And how about Duncan, do you fancy him as well?"

"He certainly is handsome and good with a thing or two I suppose." Holly was being Holly with her vague but easily seen through half-witted answers.

"That he is, I've known him as long as I can remember and there is no one of my Keepers more suitable for a husband than Duncan."

We came upon the main gate on the western wall of the castle, the vines grew thick on the unkempt exterior, and we left Perseus by the gate as the queen had commanded.

"Your father would have had a conniption if he were alive to see what has become of this place." Queen Evelyn reminisced.

"He was always the tidier of the two of you and he most certainly enjoyed his garden." Rutland was never short on bringing the bright side out of a situation that was certainly gloom.

We moved into position as Eliza moved to push the gate open. "It won't open!" The door at the gate was jammed shut.

"What do you mean it won't open Eliza?"
I said to her rather hastily.

"It is locked, barricaded, and blocked off,
we are unable to gain entry… it will not budge.
Do I need to spell it out for you!"

"Alright calm down you two no need to
get into such a fit." Rutland intervened, it would
seem these vines came in handy after all, as
he started to climb up them he looked back.
"Come on now, we don't have all night, what are
you bunch waiting for?"

"Are you off your rocker?" Holly asked.

"Not any more than his usual antics, I am
afraid." The Queen laughed. "On you go, dear."

The only problem about making it to the
top was that there was only one way down and
unfortunately it wasn't the preferred rout but it
would have to do. "Alright ladies, you see the
big pile of hay below us, just try to land softly."

"Now this is a level crazy even I won't
stand for Rutland." The Queen looked over at
him as we all dangled from the edge.

"Well it would seem you three are in need
of some encouragement." Rutland pushed the
Queen into Eliza who then grabbed onto Holly
sending all three of them flying into the hay-
stack. He unfortunately didn't fully think it
through as the fall sent a shriek out of all three
of them alerting every guard still left in the castle.

Looking down now with some audacity I asked not so politely. "Could you three move? I can't hold much longer!"

Rutland and I fell just like the rest of them, as Rutland stood up to brush himself off. Evelyn dove towards him. "Rutland! Look out!" The arrow deflected off of her sword as Eliza found the guard aiming to kill in her cross hairs, she returned fire.

"Quick Arthur to your left!" I took the guard out on the steps with one of Duncan's throwing daggers.

"Up we go!" Rutland grabbed Holly. "Stay close!"

The Queen with her sword out, lead us up the first set of stairs fearlessly. "You are certainly your daughter's mother." I whispered to her in a slight joke of admiration.

"Do you Sherwood's all talk this much?"

"Well actually..." Holly paused. "And what is it to you that we should be ourselves, even in times of despair."

"Fair enough, you are correct, nothing in this life should ever take away our identity. Thank you for the reminder."

"Doth my ears deceive my own?"

"Don't push it Rutland!"

"Come on now Eve, I was only joking."

"Eve? I haven't been called that in years!"

"I like it mum, it suits you perfectly." Eliza

moved ahead as the torches on the walls were there to guide us.

"It should be the doorway just up head." Rutland gave us all our signals to breech the throne room.

"Agnar! Are you ready to meet your maker?" Eliza burst through the door.

"MuhuhaHaHa!" A rather ghoulish figure was sitting in the throne. "You foolish child. You actually think my brother the Great King Agnar would be here on the eve of the prophecy?"

"Show yourself you coward, that throne does not belong to you!" Eve stepped in as we followed behind; the figure stood up from the shadows and stepped into the light.

"Darsus? How could you? You were our oldest friend!" The Queen seemed betrayed as an added door slammed down from above, trapping us.

"Surprise! Daddy sent me over as a young lad. Surely no one would question a child who had been saved from a shipwreck. You remember that day Rutland?"

"Enough!" Rutland yelled.

"Oh come on, let us have a little story time as it seems none of you have anywhere to be. That day you came across me floating on a piece of wood that one could only assume I was the lone survivor of a horrible shipwreck. But what you did not know was my dad planted me in your path actually after having multiple encounters with you, he knew that your compassion would make you blind to my true nature. Though it was my brother's quest for the throne, it was me who ultimately ended the reign of Findas. You were always quite the chess player Rutland but now it would seem the student has become the master." Darsus slipped out the side door as he unleashed the fiercest creature for its size in all of Findas.

"Oh well this will make for a bit of a wrinkle in our well-formed plan." The wolf like creatures pressed forward from the darkness.

"What are those things?" I asked nervously.

"Targens, they are wickedly deceptive to the mind and feed off of the blood of the unsuspecting. Best to kill them quickly as they will not let up."

"Why not just call them politicians!" I quipped to bring levity to this life and death situation.

"Holly, stay completely still!" The Targens broke from the pack moving closer breathing heavily.

"There are ten by my count, try not to miss!" Rutland encouraged.

Holly went running behind the throne which if I might add was absolutely gargantuan. The queen took the first swing as her blade cleared the jaw of the Targen rendering one less beastie. Eliza slid through the center of the room as one lunged over her in midair she took a triple-arrow out and shot it right through the heart.

Rutland with a torch in his hand fended off three of them at once as I came around the backside putting daggers into the neck of the creatures as they let out a whimpering howl. "Rutland! Arthur! Help me!" Holly was now pinned between the thrown and the wall with two Targens completely fixed on her.Rutland handed me his throwing ax from his belt.

"You see that dish suspended right above them, on my go throw this at the rope!" He moved closer towards the Targens.

"Gooooooo! Now Arthur!" I tossed that axe as hard as I could muster up the strength; it cut the rope sending oil spilling through the air.

Rutland tossed the torch he had been holding as it set the Targens a blaze it was as if they evaporated into smoke. I ran to Holly to make certain she was ok as it seemed Eliza and Eve had taken out the remaining Targen.

"Is everyone alright?" We all nodded in agreement. "Holly you can come out now!"

"One problem there were ten of them and I only counted nine of them being killed." Rutland moved his eyes towards the back of the room.

"Arthur! Behind you!" Holly screamed as she pushed the throne over, while Eliza pulled Arthur out of the way the throne crushed the tenth and final Targen.

"Thanks Holly!" I said breathing rapidly. Now we just have to figure our way out of this blasted room."

"Are you forgetting what else is in this room?"

"Merlin's door is our ticket out of here! Come on help me find it! It should be right behind this painting if memory serves me correctly." Rutland and I lifted it with all of our strength. Before realizing that it had been moved.

"He moved it actually." Eve pointed us to another wall.

"Nope! Not here either." Rutland stumped. "Maybe Agnar found it?"

Holly determined walked up to where the thrown had been pushed off its platform.

"What about this right... Here!!!" She fell through a rug the throne had been covering up.

"Holly are you ok?" Eliza ran over to her quickly. "Arthur get me a light, immediately!" She tossed it down as we stood up at the edge waiting for her to signal us. She found a second torch to light that lit a fire spiraling up a small staircase leading us down the ten-foot pit that luckily for Holly had a bed at the bottom of it. "Is this the door you were looking for?"

"Indeed it is!"

"Yes, well done dear." Eve added. "Findas shall have hope yet again."

We cleaned off the cobwebs to make sure nothing was left to chance Rutland deciphered the inscription on the lock. "May only the purest of the royal bloodline be the one who holds the true key, for it is only in their heart beat that this world may be free."

Eliza moved towards the door as she put the key into the handle only nothing extraordinary happened like before. "Well, why won't it open?"

Rutland began to pace back and forth in concentrated thought. "One moment please!" He put his hand up.

"What is he doing?" The Queen whispered to me.

"It is just how we Sherwood's process the unimaginable?"

"Alright Eliza, give me your hand."

"Excuse me but I already tried turning it with my hand!"

"Your hand please!" He insisted as he took out has blade and grazed it against her palm opening it up to bleed.

"What do you bloody think you are doing? That really freaking hurt!" Eliza pulled her hand back.

"Try turning it again."

Her bloody hand touched the knob and in an instant the blood moved through the locking mechanism of the door with all the twist and turns of a safe being opened the door swung inwards as beams of light over took our sight. We moved forward cautiously as our eyes adjusted we stumbled upon the largest time keeping instrument I have ever seen in my life.

"The Dial of Sól and Mani was said to be pure legend." Rutland was in awe. "It is believed that this very time piece is the one that gives light to the sun and on every death of the moon the process must be complete to separate the sun from its shell, giving life to a new moon." "It is called the Royal Trinity because as far back as it was made it was always supposed to remain in the hands of the royal family to make sure the process would be complete so that Findas would not fall to the darkness as it once did after the First War of the First Age." The Queen added.

"Sól and Mani? Are they of the line of Royals?" I inquired.

"Not quite, they were scientific advisors of sorts to the first Royal Family, and with the help of Merlin they built this dial which is said to contain the very first breath of creation." Eliza moved in closer. "It's much different than

I imagined, I mean mum your stories of it were fascinating, but seeing it in person is just inspirational."

"And this is supposed to bring balance to the current condition of Findas?"
Rutland pulled Holly and I aside. "Look as soon as the restoration is complete, you will find the same carved stone you struck in my house behind the bookshelves up on the second floor, as long as this door remains open you will be able to return home and if need be back directly to this very room. Promise me you will get out of here and not look back, Findas will survive on its own."

"But what about you Rutland?"

"My heart has always been in Findas, and I am afraid this is where I will remain until the end. If it should ever come for me."

Chapter 8

The room was less cluttered than the one residing in Rutland's abode but it would appear to have a second floor loaded with all kinds of interesting pieces. I understood why Merlin created such a door, its beautiful really, to have that much love for anything that you would go through all that trouble to keep it locked up with no one the wiser that you had amassed such treasures.

"Can you believe it Eve? It was right under our noses the entire time. The size of it is actually more remarkable than I imagined."

"This is what he died to protect. He had it the entire time." Said the Queen.

"Who died now? And for an oversized watch no less?" I asked unfortunately with less tact than I thought as Holly and Eliza slapped me in the back of the head at the same exact time.

"Her husband you galoot."

"My father you buffoon."

"The King of Findas!" Rutland added.

"You know for a man of your intelligence, it is surprising that you have even the slightest lapse in judgment. But nonetheless my husband King William was a man who enjoyed a good story as much as he enjoyed company with a good meal. He always talked about this dial that his father said was able to separate the heavens." She walked over to remove the covering as a sphere like object lifted from the ground freely suspended in the air it began to glow brightly.

"What in the heavens is it doing?" Rutland shouted, as the noise grew louder.

"I am not sure, but Eliza go to the eastern wall and get ready to pull the cord coming from the ceiling. Rutland you do the same at the northern wall. I will be on the western side of the room and Arthur you go to the southern wall." She looked on at Holly. "Holly my dear please wait outside the door, I am not totally sure what is going to happen."

"Holly if we don't make it out of here, you have to make it home, go right away." I yelled to her.

Holly hurried over to the doorway as we waited for the Queen's command.

"Now if any of you have anything you would like to get off of your chest, now would be the time." Rutland spoke candidly.

"I guess I will give it a go, Rutland, it was me who ran over Jefferson with my car the day after I got my license. I am sorry but he didn't run away. I did give him a proper burial if that helps."

He looked at me in a forgetful manner. "That's ok lad, I never liked that cat anyways. Always knocking over my experiments. You did me a favor with that one. I just never had the heart to put him down myself."

"Bloody hell, I felt terrible about it for years." He nodded me on as if to say, is that all, we face life or death and you chose to tell me about my cat.

"Eve I know we never say it and I know it's because I repress any notion of feelings I have but I love you, with all my heart, I love you." It was the first time in my entire life I heard those words come from Rutland's mouth, he even had me choked up.

"Looks like I guess I will give it a chance." Eliza seemed unsure of what she wanted to say.

"Rutland, you practically raised me and mum everything that I have become is from your sacrifice. I know it couldn't have been easy to let me go. And Arthur the short time I have known you, well you are not too bad yourself."

"Aw sweetheart, lets finish this therapeutic discussion another time, shall we?" The room was almost filled with the light as we could barely see one another. "Immediately after you pull the cord run for the door." Yelled the Queen.

We all pulled at the same exact time as four claw-like needles came up from the floor. All but one of them had pierced the sphere.

"Go now run for the door, it will not contain the energy much longer." Rutland pushed all three of us through the doorway.

"Rutland no, you will surely die, come with us now."

"Arthur what is Rutland doing?"

"The dial jammed, I fear he is going to try and complete the process himself."

Looking into the abyss with chaos surrounding him his heart remained open and his eyes still hopeful. Rutland disappeared into the light as the fourth arm pierced the sphere, I could see his smile and nod through the uncertainty of it all, the room concealed most of the energy as the rest leaked into the stairwell the sound could be heard for miles. By the time we were to gain our consciousness back, Rutland was gone but the ninth moon had been fully restored.

"Rutland, you idiot! There had to have been another way!" The queen cried out as we all mourned his loss.

"Mum I am afraid there was no other way to complete the Royal Trinity. The sphere had to be punctured by four." Eliza put her hand on the shoulder of her grieving mother.

"Eliza, give her some room." I asked her for a brief moment. "Look, Rutland's last request was for Holly and myself to go home immediately after the completion of the trinity but as long as the door remains open, I can come back or even stay if you want me to. I just need to get Holly back home where she belongs."

"Rutland is right you must go. My mum and I will meet up with the other Keepers to finish off Agnar and Darsus. Findas owes you more than a bit of gratitude and one day when we meet again beyond the stars I will repay the kindness you have shown me." She said as we gazed into each other's eyes.

"Arthur, hurry up we must go before anyone finds us, I am sure by now that King what's his face or his smug nosed brother has sent someone back to how should I put this, kill us. I for one have no plans on dying today."

"One more thing before I go." I pulled Eliza close as I knew that in life and in love the chance to kiss the one you are crazy about for the first time only comes but once in a life time in this world or the next.

"Eliza we must leave at once and leave no trace of this room. Arthur, use the swords on the wall to find your way home. God speed."

They were gone just like that. "We save their entire world and no one will ever know. And what are we going to do about Rutland?"

"Well honestly we could just say he passed away and requested cremation." Holly putting her more deceitful side to use.

"Yeah, that could actually work but first we must find the swords for the carved stone." We found our way to the top rafter overlooking the room and as Rutland said it would be the same hand carved stone that was in his room, was right behind the shelves. "Here you go, take a good swing and if all goes as planned we will be back in London before anyone becomes the wiser."

"Arthur I know this all has been a lot to take in but if this what it took to get us back to being friends, I would do it all over again in a heartbeat."

"Holly, you are not my friend, those I can

choose when and if I want them but you are however my family and I wouldn't trade that in for the world. Now how about we head home before one of us sheds a tear."

We struck the stone and off to home wewere as all I could think of was Eliza and how much they still had to do in Findas. We landed back into the room that started it all. Still dazed from the travel I gently tapped Holly. "Come on we need to get you up now. No time to waste."

"Oh but I am exhausted and I just want to stay on this strangely comfy floor." She moaned.

"Then I guess I am just going to have to complete Rutland's last plan alone."

"What are you going on about now Arthur? You have to let him go, Rutland is gone."

"He may be gone but before he went, he handed me this piece of paper."

"Oh alright but only if you promise me we are not going back to Findas. I just want to shower and…"

"Holly if we don't find whatever it is Rutland wrote down on this piece of paper, there may not be a Findas to go back to. They may not be in eternal darkness but without this item I fear they may never defeat Agnar."

"Well, what is it then? Let's have a look." She sat up and demanded.

"I am not quite sure all it says 'Reuel'"

"Well it would seem there was more to it

but I am afraid you tore it coming back to London" Holly pointed out the jagged edge of the paper where it appeared more writing was to be.

"Look if we are going to make this happen we need to get our barring straight." I moved usquickly to the front door where I had assumed the newspaper would be so we could figure out what day it was, I thought that there would be a pile of them by now but to my surprise there was none.

"Can you see what time it is?"

"It would appear to be a shade past five in the evening." She called out from the living room.

I saw one of our neighbors pulling in from work. "Excuse me sir, this is going to sound like a silly question but do you know what day it is?"

"It is Monday?" He said with a certain befuddlement.

"And the Date?"

"It is the First of May. Are you feeling alright?"

"Actually quite fine thank you very much. Enjoy your evening." I rushed back into the house.

"Arthur, What is it? Are you ok?" Holly followed me to Rutland's bedside. "Hello! Arthur? Are you going to let me into what is going on inside that brain of yours?"

"Well our cover is still good as it is only the first of May and…"

"That is not possible, are you saying that time just stood practically still while we were in Findas?"

"No, what I am saying is that somehow there, days do not last as long as ours and given the rotation of Findas is opposite of ours it would appear that time simply did not pass us by here as much as I thought."

"Ok forgive me for asking but what next?"

"First we need to get rid of Rutland's body double I believe that our uncle kept a spare open grave in the yard for such an occasion."

"And then?"

"Then we need to find an urn and fill it with dirt so it will pass at the funeral which you are going to need to notify the family" We started wheeling the bed out of the room as carrying the dead weight throughout the house was not an option. I am pretty sure that this wasn't even a real body but just in case I thought it was best to leave it with some dignity.

"And when shall I set the funeral for?"

"Tomorrow night I will be back before you know it. I know you don't want me to go but I need you to handle the family just in case any of them decide to pop by unannounced."

"I can most certainly take care of that."

She finished putting the last bit of dirt on the grave before heading inside to find the perfect urn while I tried to make heads or tails of the torn note Rutland handed me.

"I am no genius myself but your calculations are wrong."

"What are you talking about, those are based on the facts, they are not wrong." "That would make Queen Evelyn like thousands of years old. What if time and space are not affected because their world defies all laws and theories of physics in our world?"

"That would be considered magic, make believe, and I simply cannot operate on the basis of a fairytale."

"You need to wake up Arthur, you are currently in one and you certainly seem to be fighting hard for your happily ever after, if I have ever been told a bed time story or two by Uncle Rutland."

"Just please go find an urn and fill it with some dirt."

"Oh but I have and I hope you don't mind I used a bit from the flower pot on the front stoop."

"Lovely you picked his least favorite container and I guess it doesn't matter much now that he really is gone, but he did say not to touch that flower pot."

"There wasn't even a flower in it! It is literally a pot of soil."

"I know, I know but it was his pot of soil. Is all." I reminded her as she continued on about Rutland.

"You know what I think?" She said presumptuously. "I think you are in love and with good reason. Eliza is perfect for you."

"Go on then." I let her continue.

"It is like Rutland use to say 'Anything is possible if you can find it in your heart to carry on.' I added the last part but you understand the point."

"You my dear are all too perfect." I ran over and kissed her on her forehead as she was engraving Rutland's initials on the outside of his least favorite vase on account of it was from his first and only wife who he married for any reason but love.

"What on earth did I do?" Holly wondered.

"No time to explain I have to find Reuel." As I went back behind Merlin's door where she followed close behind.

"Did you actually think I would let you look for whatever it is we are currently looking for alone?"

"Well no but I didn't think an invite was necessary as I figured you would follow anyways."

"I will pretend you didn't just make fun of

me after all we have come through the past couple of well whatever they were, days or hours."

"We are looking for the Heart of the King!"

"Now you have officially lost me."

"It is not an actual heart but said to be the most prize possession of the King, it is a sword of sorts."

"Oh right yes of sorts, so it's not completely a sword but it could be a sword."   "Legend has it and by legend I mean Rutland use to speak of it all the time and he referred to it as the Heart of the King, its blade has the ability to bring judgment upon anyone it pierces and will protect its bearer for all of eternity as long as the bearer upholds its honor."

"And you got all of this from the word Reuel?"

"No actually, I got this from you. When you brought up finding the impossible."

"Right and what does it actually look like? Have you ever seen it before?"

"The blade is three feet long and its handle is built for speed, also there should be a marking of some sort indicating its owner.

My guess would be, it belonged to the King of Findas and he then passed it on to Rutland to insure its survival. Either way we must find it before it is too late."

"We better get our search on then if you

are to get back and save the day, and hopefully get the girl."

We examined every inch of the room, high and low until Holly bumped into one of the suits of armor that was upright against the wall.

"Be careful now he got that armor from the Holy land the last time he was there, it was from the crusades, surely a one of a kind artifact."

"I was being careful, the armor was not mounted properly!" She claimed as she started to stack it back up on the stand it fell from.

"And make sure that you wipe it for any dust. You know Rutland will haunt us from beyond if any of his things were to become filthy, especially his armor collection."

"Ummm, Arthur I think you should come see this." She raised the sword up as the bottom of the blade towards the handle read the word Reuel and on the other side it translated to 'Friend of God'.

I knew in that moment that the only way to set things right was to return to Findas with the Sword of Reuel and kill Agnar myself for revenge is not fit for a future queen and her heart would never fully recover from such an act. So, I strapped the sword around my shoulder and prepared myself to go back.

"If I am not back by the funeral please fill

a second urn for me." I said jokingly.

"Don't you dare, say that! Arthur Clive Sherwood!" Holly hit me in the arm. "Please come back to us, your family needs you more than ever. I need you now more than ever"

"I promise you that I will be back before you know it. Just please make sure that no one is the wiser and if anyone tries to visit, well you know what to do." In that very instant, the doorbell rung louder than usual, giving me a good scare. "You have to be kidding, please go see who it is."

She pulled the door wide open. "Aunt Pip, what a pleasant surprise? I was just on my way out. Arthur and Eliza have decided to take a mini-holiday, so I was just over to tidy up a bit."

"So you and Arthur are getting along well with the wedding planning and all?"

"More than you can imagine, but I am late for my evening class, do forgive me for the briefness of this conversation."

"No worries dearie." She squeezed Holly almost to a burst. "I am just glad to see you two getting along again, after all these years."

"Indeed it has been like old times."

"I don't mean to pry but where did you say they were off to?"

"To a little cottage up north for some rest and recuperation, I believe she said it was long overdue and about time Arthur got out from behind his desk for a change."

"She is right you know, never could get his father out from behind the desk and now it seems Arthur has found a little more balance in his life." She tried to push through the threshold of the door. "And how is Rutland doing? If you ask me I think Arthur should just pull the plug, not that I don't love him but he has lived many lives over."

"Would you look at that, it is time to go! I still need to wash up before school tonight! I will just need to lock up now. I will see you on Thursday yeah?"

"Alright no need to be all jittery. Everything ok? You look like you've been through a war cleaning this house!"

"You have know idea Aunt Pip how right you are! I would tell you all about it but I just really cannot be late for this class." Holly did a splendid job ushering my mum out the door. She even pulled her car down the block until the coast was clear and then she doubled back to the house.

"Maybe you are more like Rutland than I." We shared a good laugh.

"Your mum is so sweet but my goodness please if I am ever that nosey, would you let me know?"

"It would be my honor, now if I am not back by Wednesday you have to close off Merlin's door and promise me to never open it again."

"And on a serious note, what do I tell the family of your whereabouts?"

"Tell them anything but the truth or they will lock you up in the loony bin for sure."

"You know how bad I am at lying."

"True, ok, new plan go into where I was sleeping, my top desk drawer and grab the envelope addressed to my parents. All the answers they need; will be in it."

"Why wasn't this our first plan?"

"Just don't mess up the house too much while I am gone. Love you Holly-O!"   "Right back at you Artie." She placed her hands up into a half a heart and I completing it with mine like we were kids all over again.

As the nostalgia wore off, she said her tear filled hopeful goodbye before I struck the stone yet again pulling me back into the Lost Kingdom of Findas in hopes that I am not too late.

Chapter 9

I busted down the staircase, landing on my feet for the first time. "Finally, you are starting to get the hang of this." I laughed dusting myself off.

That was when the whisper started. "Arthur, you cannot let Eliza or her mother kill Agnar."

"Rutland is that you?" I spun around with the sword in hand thinking I might be losing my mind, but the voice continued.

"Revenge is not the path of the righteous, for if the new kingdom is built upon such an act surely it will fall again."

"Show yourself!" I exhausted, fearing that the trip back to Findas had taken its toll on my soul.

"You must be the one to free them from this treachery." The voice echoed.

"Don't leave me, Rutland I need you here."

"I am sorry my dear boy, my time has come. This is your cross to bear."

Fear over took my heart but still I moved forward as I knew Rutland had his eye on me from where ever it maybe he wandered to next.

The first daylight of the tenth moon lit Findas up as the ninth sun found its place in the sky. The castle walls seemed more open and the hope flooding this land was palpable. Still with caution I proceeded to the western gate, where I could hear scratching from the other side. I hit the lever up like raising the curtain for a magician's big reveal.

"Perseus! I told you I would come back for you!" I ran over to him as if I raised him from a pup. "You ready to ride in and save the day?" He bowed as I saddled up like the man Rutland always knew I could be.

We moved thoroughly to a higher look out point from within the border of the Inner Lands. Searching for a place of entry, a group of soldiers from the High Cliffs surrounded by the knights of Agnar came directly into our view, so we came to their aid. Like clockwork Perseus tore through them limb by limb, as I put my daggers to work. The dust finally settled.

"Have any of you seen the Keepers?" They looked at me in fear. "Can you point me in the direction of Queen Evelyn or her daughter Princess Eliza?"

They shook their heads, "I am sorry sir but they are currently in no man's land."

"I beg your pardon?"

"The heart of the war, Akemi and Hachiro lead the last charge before sun rise. They have not returned for we fear that no one will return."

"How many of you are there left, able to fight?"

"Unfortunately we are what is left for now, that is until the wounded heal."

"And just where might we find these wounded warriors?"

"Take me with you, I will show you the way to the camp!" the strongly shaped man stepped out from the rest as I gave him the hand up onto Perseus.

"Oh delightful, and you are?" we continued the greeting on our way to the camp.

"My name is Eno, I was a fisherman in the sea of Idunn before the war started."

"It is a pleasure to meet you, I was a lawyer in London a week ago, and most call me Arthur." I realized my profession was not easily recognized in Findas and rightfully so.

"Do you think we have an actual chance at defeating Agnar?"

"It will take nothing short of a miracle and though logic tells me otherwise, I believe in my heart of hearts that we must try."

"The camp is just up there on the other side of that rock formation."

I will never get used to being surrounded by the extensions of war. The moans of the dying and scoffs of the victors, The weeping of widows or of the mothers and fathers who lost a son or daughter, to the not knowing if I will ever rise with the sun ever again. Though this time was dark, it was nothing a familiar face couldn't cure.

"Althia, have you heard from Finlay or any of the other Keepers it is quite urgent?"

"Oh it is so good to see your face Arthur, I heard about Rutland as well but no nothing from Finlay or anyone from the Shadoway for that matter."

"Do you know of anyone who is able to fight?"

"Look around you! We are backed up already with more coming in by the hour."

"I can see that but if I told you I have a

plan to put an end to all of this madness."

"Well, why didn't you lead with that in the first place?"

"I am going to show you something but you cannot tell anyone, anonymity is going to be our one true ally in this endeavor."

"Go on then show me what you have there." I pulled the sword from its sheath.

"It can't be!" She gasped. "It is the sword of the First King of Findas."

"You've seen it before?"

"No most certainly not but it is said that the creator of Findas forged that sword on the day the First King was anointed over the land. It was an olive branch, so to speak. Up until right now it was said to have been lost."

"Rutland you beautiful man you." I interrupted. "I am sorry, please, by all means continue."

"The sword of Reuel it was called by those who spoke of it but to those who held it, know it only as the Heart of the King. This is the sword that is said to give redemption to Findas; the bearer will bring about the end to the reign of Agnar. Do you know what this means?"

"That we are about to do something crazy?"

"No, no but yes, this means that you truly are the man from beyond the stars, like the prophecy spoke of so long ago."

"You must have me confused for someone else."

"No I knew it the day you walked into the Shadoway, call it a mother's intuition. Now what is this plan of yours and how many able body people will you be in need of."

"Five give or take, really all depends on how able."

"We have three for sure that I released this morning, you make four and I would make five."

"No way am I letting you come with us. Finlay would have my head on a spear if something were to happen to you."

"I will have you know Arthur, I wasn't always at home raising my family. In fact it was my ability to handle a blade that caught Finlay's eye in the first place. That and I beat him in a couple jousting tournaments growing up."

"That may be so, but do you still think you have all of your old moves."

She flipped the sword lying on the ground beside the soldier she was tending to and before I knew it, the tip was pitted ever so gently into my rib.

"Right you are then, let's go no time to forget now."

"Let's" She moved her arm leading the way towards the other able body fighters. Which to my eyes were about the most unfit for

160

the job, making them perfect for the task.

"Up you stand, look alive. We have one chance to get this right and not all of us may make it out alive I am afraid. But I promise you this, none of us will ever be forgotten." "What is it exactly that we will be doing?"

"First who is able to swing a sword besides Althia?" No hands were raised. "Splendid! It looks like Althia, you will be with me."

"I will fight until the death if necessary."

"Thank you but your death will most certainly bring about my death, so let us try to stay alive. You three will help us lift the castle's main gate and then man the arrow cannon's along the front wall."

"Done! Anything for Findas!"

"Lastly we are going to charge from behind as by now the castle has been completely depleted of any guards. Agnar as well as Darsus are presumably on the front line currently"

"And just how are we going to get to Agnar and Darsus?"

"The cannon fire should cause a good stir from the army and as they are looking up. We will be riding through the ranks on the back of Perseus cloaked by this blanket I found, of course."

"Are you mad? I am not stepping foot on that Drak'on!"

"He has himself a Drak'on?"

"His name is Perseus! Thank you very much and he will lead us to Agnar, as his sense of smell is heightened during meal time which is roughly in the next hour, so we need to go now."

Perseus was pacing at the gate with Althia and myself strapped to its back underneath the blanket that blended so perfectly into his skin. "Are you ready for this?" I stuck my hand out from beneath the covering to signal the raising of the gate. I heard his footsteps moving back to position one on the tower wall as the gate finished opening. The cannon fire sounded and you could hear the ropes attached to the arrows taking out swarms of soldiers. Perseus took off like a horse down the track. We both held on for dear life.

"On my go, at the ready! Hold! Hold! Now!" We jumped off Perseus as we started taking out every single one of Agnar's soldiers that stood in our way.

"That's enough!" A man with evil in his eyes and a crook in his smile moved towards the two of us.

"You must be Agnar."

"You have heard of me and yet I do not know who you are exactly."

"Arthur Clive Sherwood."

"And yet still I have never heard of you!"

"Agnar, quit fooling around and just end

162

this poor excuse of a life." Darsus stepped out from the other side.

"So nice of you to join us brother. I would say you can have the woman but maybe I should let this be a fair fight and let them both of have a go at me" he mocked.

The sword was swung and like that we were engaged in full on combat. "You do realize my men will never let it come even close to my death, surrender now and I will maybe spare your lives."

I came out at him with my smaller daggers using them to shield the blow from his axe and sword. Althia went directly after Darsus without warning and knocked him to his hind side.

"Feisty you are, I will most certainly enjoy this." His enjoyment was short lived as Althia put her blade right through his chest.

"You stupid foolish woman!" Agnar went after Althia with all of his anger as Perseus rode in to bring her out of the chaos. It was now just, Agnar and me, two strangers willing to kill each other for honor. That was until my boot was struck with an arrow keeping me from moving. "Eliza, what on earth are you doing?"

"Agnar is mine."

"No he is ours!" The queen backed up her daughter.

"Well this is just brilliant! Three for the

price of one, does it get any better than this? I had my most formidable spies searching all over Findas for you and now both of you have come to find me!"

"I am afraid that this is not a three for one deal but rather a one for one!"

"Oh yes you are correct I am going to start with Arthur and finish with you!"

I pulled the sword from its holder cutting through the arrow that had me pinned and without hesitation I pushed the blade of my sword through Agnar's heart. He took a breath in as he recognized the blade that brought about his demise. "Impossible!" He fell upon his knees.

Eliza approached him. "Bow before your Queen!"

"Never!" He took his last breath as we turned to the more immediate threat. It seemed we were in a no way out situation. One by one the Knights of Agnar took their shots at us. That was until on top of the horizon stood Duncan, Hachiro, Akemi, Althia, Fergus, Finlay and the army of the Hills of Halle rushing towards us bringing the war on all fronts had worked.

"Sorry for the delay!" Duncan began fighting everyone in his path.

"Better late than never!" The queen said standing back to back with the rest of us.

"So Arthur you want to explain what my wife is doing in the battlefield?"

"Well Finlay, actually I um can explain that." As I was not finding my words, she put her sword past Finlay's head and into the face of one of the men who was just about to kill him.

"Have you forgot that I taught you how to use a blade or two?"

"Love you too honey!"

"Now is not really the time to argue over who wears the pants sweetheart? Let's try and make it home to our son!"

"You should listen to your wife Finlay!" I added.

Fergus and Hachiro were trading blows with about twelve attackers at once. As per usual Akemi stepped in to finish them off.

The Keepers fought like a fine oiled machine and Agnar's remaining leaders surrendered by night fall and those who had ravaged this land were banished once more this time to the unforgiving sea to the south of Findas.

"Hachiro?" The queen summoned.

"Yes, Your, Majesty."

"Can your bird get a message to all the tribes?"

"Yes anything at all!"

"Tell them it is time to come home! Findas is restored and tonight we will feast!"

We returned to the castle that night and

tore down every last remaining shred of Agnar and his people. We tossed it to the fire pile just inside the courtyard. The music was loud and the cheer was perfect but still my mind was troubled. It would seem news in Findas travelled fast as the entire Kingdom, wanderers and all celebrated across the land.

"And then Rutland fell into the horses' droppings." Laughter was all that could fill the throne room tonight as we reminisced on Rutland's adventures in Findas.

"To those we love that we have lost! May, they always be found within our hearts." I raised my glass as the rest of the Keepers enjoyed the spoils of victory.

"Come dance with me Arthur!"

We stood toe to toe and shifted to the lovely sounds of the people. "So what now?"

"Will you stay here with me?" she asked.

"I won't." She seemed dejected by my response.

"I will go wherever you go for as long as I live." I got down on one knee. "Eliza Joanne Dunmore. Will you come back to London with me and let me take you on a proper date?"

"I am not sure that is going to work."

"Is that so?"

"Nothing about us is proper, but if you would like to take me to dinner, that would be lovely."

The next morning the sun got up particularly early and we readied ourselves for the journey home, not before receiving a royal parade of sorts through the dining hall.

"Arthur it has been a pleasure, please take care of my daughter for one day you will return as king and queen." We moved towards the staircase below the throne.

"Duncan! Come here it is time my daughter got a Keeper of her own! Please send my love to Holly!"

"You mean I am going with them!"

"True love does not know time and nor can it be contained by any amount of space, so please go, and listen to your heart."

Eliza looked back at her mother. "Are you sure mother?"

"Go on dear. Findas will be ready for you when you return and I promise you that you will be too, you have already proven yourself fit to be queen. For now however there is no doubt in my mind that your current home, is beyond the stars with that man over there who came all the way back here just to make sure you were alright."

Chapter 10

In a whirlwind we entered into the room stumbling to our feet we heard water running in the kitchen then her voice called.   "Arthur is that you?"

I looked at Duncan to go on ahead and surprise Holly. "You know, we really should put a lock on that room!"

She turned around dropping the plate currently in her hand. "Duncan! But what in the dickens are you even doing here?" She ran into his arms, as Eliza and I watched from the door what appeared to be their first kiss.

"My mum figured I could use a Keeper of my own and thought that Duncan would be the perfect one to come back with me."

"Eliza! I am most delighted that you are here as well and just in time too, Arthur, I was about to have you both declared missing!"

Not even ten minutes back and there was already a ring at the door and before I could answer, my mother busted down the door. "What are you lot waiting for the service for Rutland is in twenty minutes and you three look like you have just been in a war?" We all rolled our eyes in amusement as Duncan walked into the room.

"I couldn't find the bath, so I just went outside, I hope you don't mind" We tried to waive him off from anymore awkward talk.

"And just who are you, and that outfit, is rather strange?"

"I am Duncan Ma'am, very pleased to meet you."

"Aunt Pip this is my boyfriend. The one I told you about." Holly did her best to convince her.

"That's lovely dear very nice but you lot better go hurry up and get ready. Where are his ashes?"

"On the table!" We rushed upstairs to wash up. The girls ran to Eliza's room as I rushed to find Duncan and myself some suitable clothes for this occasion.

"Is it a usual ritual to dress up when burying the dead?" Duncan had so much to learn if he was to have any chance of surviving in this world.

"Here, just try this on!" he dropped trout right in front of me before I pointed him in the direction of the bathroom. "You may change in here and also this is the proper place to do your business." I nodded, as he seemed to understand.

"Well what do you think? Will Holly be impressed?"

"She most certainly will be Duncan."

"I even found room for my daggers."

"About that, it may be best to leave them at home for now."

"But a Keeper must never be without his weapon."

"That may be so in Findas, but in London it is preferable that we settle our quarrels like gentleman and if need be a punch or two."

"So no blades?"

"No blades!"

We found our way downstairs where my mother was impatiently waiting for us. "All grown up and you still need your mother to help make sure you are not late. By the way have you seen his ashes? Filthy, they could have at least bathed the man before burning him up."

"Mum have a little decency, the man has barely been dead three days!"

Holly whispered in my ear as we were out the door. "She isn't completely wrong about how DIRTy he is."

"That's an entire other level of wrong, just wrong." We shared a private laugh.

We walked into the old creaky church, as it was Rutland's wish to have his service there. He often told me how it was his home away from home; he would sit in these pews for hours unbothered by the silence.

Within an hour the room was filled with condolences and sorrow, the Reverend addressed the family first and loved ones next as Rutland counted us all his friends.

"I have known Rutland almost as long as his own mother. We were inseparable so to speak. But seeing all of you here today I know that though he may not currently be with us, his memory won't soon be forgotten. The floor is now open to any who wish to speak on his behalf."

My dad oddly enough was the first to stand as he made his way down to the front of the room that was minimally decorated with a simple picture of Rutland and his least favorite container that well only Holly and myself knew that he wasn't quite in there.

He cleared his throat. "Hello all, thank

you so much for coming here today as we honor the life of Rutland Quincy Sherwood.

My name is Brunley Sherwood, when my father passed away, it was Rutland who stepped in and raised, my siblings and I, alongside my mother. He didn't have to do that but he was the type of man you never had to ask for help, it was always in him to be that for those he loved dearly. He taught me how to tie my first tie, and gave me my first job after school. He always said, 'Brunley if you take away anything from our time together, always be a giver and a keeper. Give all of your heart to those you love and keep those you love in all of your heart. Give of your time equally so and keep your priorities in order. Lastly give unto this world your very best for it owes you nothing in return and keep your head high always, as it's much easier to navigate your failures looking up than it is not looking at all." He pulled a handkerchief from his pocket and began to sniffle. "I will always hold you in my heart."

I stood to my feet to console him as Holly found herself now at the front. "Hi there, I am Holly Martin, and many of you may not know this about me but as a child I spent a fair bit of time at Uncle Rutland's house. I remember once having cookies for breakfast and how he was a masterful bedtime story teller. Actually he could tell you a story no matter the time of day as he had more than enough to last him ten lifetimes over. The best part of being at Rutland's was nothing could get you down, when you walked through that door you were greeted with such overwhelming joy that all of life's problems discappeared as he used to say. I am surely glad that I had such precious moments with him for it makes today feel less like a loss and more like a gain, as seeing each and every one of you here only confirms what I already believed to be true of Rutland."

One by one and even some came as a couple, recounting stories, some of which may indeed have been legend turned reality. The last remaining of his crew went and surely it was my turn to finish off the service properly, only Eliza grabbed my hand and cut right in.
Standing nervously her voice shook throughout the room.

"I know you all are probably wondering who on earth I am. My name is Eliza Dunmore and like many of you I have known Rutland for some time now. He was a teacher of the extraordinary, a believer in the impossible and a doer of his word. Most of all he was a friend and without whom I would have never met my Fiancé Arthur or his lovely cousin Holly to that I owe so much already. Days like today, remind myself of why Rutland held family so near and dear to his heart. Take away your vocation, lose your possessions, forget your dreams but keep your family near and everything in this world will be right."

I wasn't sure how I was going to follow that up as there wasn't a dry eye in the place but as Rutland would tell me you need to give it a go anyways.

"Where to begin? Rutland was Rutland he never asked for much but left you with more than you need, of whatever it was he had. Call it gumption, call it exuberance, passion, love, humility, and grace his very presence was contagious. Not once can I remember him yelling in displeasure. He enjoyed learning as much as he enjoyed teaching others about his travels. He could tie any knot, speak multiple languages, decode puzzles and riddles, he once memorized the entire book of Proverbs just so if he was ever met with uncertainty he had the wisdom within his heart to maneuver it with ease. He sailed all seven seas, has landed on every continent twice and then some, mountains he has climbed them all, deserts he has wandered most, and still not a single river on this earth that he himself hasn't navigated. He was ninety-six by the count of his age, his heart however put him easily in his mid-forty's and yet his experience clocked him in at least five hundred and eighty six. He loved you all dearly, he once told me that life was too short to not love everyone we encounter, even if that encounter is unfavorable."

The Reverend took back over and closed out the ceremony. We had an enjoyable meal at my parents' house with all the siblings and close family. Then Eliza, Duncan, Holly and myself returned to Rutland's where we decided it best to share the responsibilities in caring for his home. Walking up the drive as Eliza put the key in the door, I looked towards the pot of soil and to my surprise a flower had indeed sprouted up with blue pedals and royal red tips, I smiled in disbelief.

"Do you all see it to?" I had to make sure I wasn't losing my marbles.

"Truly magnificent, you know what that is?" Duncan exhaled.

"I do indeed."

As the three of them went to prepare their rooms for bedtime, I moved towards Rutland's study and sat right in his chair which I pulled up to his desk.

Eliza walked into the room. "Are you doing ok Arthur?"

"I am quite well... my Fiancé?"

"Yeah, well the way I see it there was no need to go backwards since Holly started the wedding planning already!"

"That is certainly efficient as you are not one for small talk!"

"Why not just dive into the deep end? Am I right?" She kissed me goodnight and left me with my thoughts.

Thinking nothing of it, I pulled the center drawer open. "Impossible" I pondered. Holding up the very container of ink I brought for Rutland to Findas. Staring at the object in bewilderment of what possibilities it held, I couldn't help but say aloud as if he was in the room. "You truly are the Incredible Mr. Rutland Quincy Sherwood."

The End... For now.

To my loving Father who could make the simplest of incidents into the grandest of tales. To my loving mother who was the voice of every bed time story I had ever heard. To my Loving wife who has given me the gift of both deep friendship and fatherhood, I adore you all.

- D.R.

Continue the journey of a lifetime with The Finder's Keep Part Two "Rutland Quincy Sherwood's Unbelievable Guide to Salvaging the Impossible"